Taste This, America

by Chef Victor

First edition.

ISBN: 9780578535852

Instagram: @a_united_state_of_mind

Taste This, America!

Let's make America palatable again.

Taste, smell, sight, touch, and judgement are the key senses we need to use when making a masterful meal. It's of utmost importance that we use these inherited traits to create wellness for ourselves and the generations who follow. In part, this is accomplished by the means of carefully designed dishes.

We've included 42 wonderful meals and preparations representing Title 42 of the United States Code that addresses civil rights, the health of our public, and the welfare of our American people.

Enjoy!

By the way, if you see any typos or mistakes, let me know. I'm a fucking chef, not a writer.

Kitchen Table of Contents

Chapter 1

Breakfast

Traitor eggs
(includes influence from Canada and United Kingdom)

Ingredients

The holiday sauce
3 egg yolks; for a guide on how to efficiently separate the yellow from the white please go to www.lockthemupforpearlharbor.com
1/14 teaspoon spicy mustard
1 tablespoon yellow lemon juice
0.5 (this is a half) cup butter, the real stuff

The Benedict eggs—these are not named after that Wall Street dude, but after the traitor, which we all think it's named after anyway
6 slices bacon from a Canadian pig
1 tablespoon butter
1 English muffin, white not wheat
4 large egg whites from white or brown eggs; remember that traitors come in all colors
1 tablespoon white vinegar
Salt
White pepper

Instructions

Here's how you make the holiday sauce: in an American-made blender, combine egg yolks, mustard, and lemon juice. Whip that muthafucka till smooth. Put the butter in a separate microwave safe container and microwave till melted. The microwave was invented by our pal and American engineer Percy Spencer after we kicked ass in World War II. Turn the blender back on and slowly pour in some of that delicious hot butter. The sauce will thicken.

OK, let's make the rest of this breakfast: heat a small skillet over medium high heat. Melt some more real butter. Cook, don't brown, the Canadian bacon. Bring a large US-factory produced pot of salted water to a boil. Don't forget to toast those bastard English muffins. Put the vinegar into your boiling water. Gently slide the egg whites from the eggs you cracked open into the boiling water, single file. Cover the pot and turn off the heat, letting the eggs poach for 5 minutes. Fetch the poached eggs from the water. And speaking of poaching, there is some serious poaching of our American youth by the evil masters who want to change our beautiful country into a pile of blah. See, we all have a fundamental human need to belong to something. The "changers" know this and have infiltrated the minds of our youth to make them believe that they do not "belong" to this great country, and therefore need to thwart the existing presence of our great nation, turn their minds against hard-working, rule-following, successful Americans, and create their own world. Which is a bunch of bull, because they just want followers who won't question their intentions, but will doubt in the beauty of our United States. They want to create traitors. The problem is, the backbone of America is too strong. It may bend a little as these traitors come up with new and sneaky modes to try to subdue our greatness, but our backbone will never break. Americans belong to America. Period. On to the presentation. I'm getting hungry!

Presentation

Get a plate and gently place the flakey English muffin and the non-committal Canadian bacon on it. These countries' products belong on the bottom. Distribute the slices of bacon in any type of symbol you deem necessary. You can even make a miniature Eiffel Tower or some famous structure from Canada or Ireland (if they have any). Slide the poached egg on top and pour some sauce on top. Eat up! You're gonna need some utensils to eat this crap like an opened-face sandwich. Or you can put another English muffin half on top and eat it like a regular American sandwich. Maybe you don't have anything to do today except get your free check from the government. Maybe you have to call around and get an extension on all of your loans and bills, because you don't friggin pay them on time. If that's the case, take your time and eat it open faced with your fancy silverware. While you're at it, throw on your favorite fake news exploitation channel. Don't worry, us hard-working citizens of the USA will take care of your selfish and always-needy ways. If you have a job to actually go to, like a real American, make that sucker into a sandwich and woof it down. Get out there and kick ass today. You have the moral integrity of our country to defend.

Unpretentious ham and egg bake

Ingredients

8 eggs; remember, brown eggs are not better than white eggs

1 thick slice of Virginia ham

This is a country ham, made in Virginia, from pigs that were raised in Virginia, sliced by an American butcher. Of course, there's no USDA statute that legally requires what one calls a Virginia-style ham to be made in the actual state. You'd probably insult someone or hurt someone's feelings. Ugh! So, you better make sure and check the gosh damn label or ask your butcher if you got the right kind.

1 white onion

1 cup shredded cheddar cheese; do it yourself from a block of cheese, not that processed crap. Make America Grate Again.

3 tablespoons butter from a cow

Salt

Pepper

1/2 teaspoon dried tarragon

1 pinch dried thyme

Some slices of white bread

Probably anywhere from 4 to 20

Instructions

Preheat your oven to 350 degrees. Get your eggs and crack the egg yolks and whites into a bowl and beat with a hammer (just kidding) till nice and frothy. Toss in the salt, pepper, tarragon, and thyme. If you don't have the last two, screw it. Your egg dish will be great without them. They're not common spices and don't really help anything. Some high society people try to make you feel like you need unheard of food enhancers in your pantry to be a good cook. Babble. In the meantime, cut that ham into small cubes about a half-inch wide. Peel the skin off the onion (duh) and finely slice it. That means cut it in really small pieces, not "hey, do a fine job slicing that onion." Heat up a frying pan on medium with a little butter. Cook up the ham pieces and onions till they're just browned a little. Once they're black, they're no good. Mix together the eggs and spices, ham and onions, and cheese in a large bowl and stir up a bit. Pour egg mixture into a greased 8-inch-square baking dish. Bake at 350 degrees for 40-45 minutes, or till eggs are cooked and set.

Presentation

Just before the egg bake is done, start the toast. Put white bread slices into a toaster. If you have company, put someone in charge of the toast, as there are many series of bread toasting that will be needed. Now, not all people are cut out to be great chefs, but I sure hope everyone can make toast without messing it up. If they can't, they don't belong in your house. This is called cutting the fat or more recently "draining the swamp" (if you didn't know what that meant). Get your breakfast plates ready. Cut the egg bake into nice squares. Serve with toast and butter. Simple breakfast. Everyone's happy.

The greatest country breakfast

Ingredients

6 eggs
1/2 pound pork sausage
1/4 cup chopped yellow onion
1/3 cup whole milk
2 tablespoons minced fresh parsley
1/4 teaspoon salt
1/2 cup shredded cheddar cheese
1 and 1/2 cups ~~frozen shredded hash brown potatoes~~
   (Don't be a putz. Make your own fucking hash
   browns.)
1 pound russet potatoes, peeled
1/2 teaspoon salt
1/4 teaspoon garlic powder
1/4 teaspoon onion powder
1/4 cup extra-virgin olive oil

Instructions

Crumble the pork sausage and put it in a pre-heated, cast-iron skillet. Cook on medium heat till all the pink is removed. Relax. This is not toxic masculinity. Ya, that's a term I heard rumbling around the left circle of failure. Pink does not represent anything. It's just a damn color.

When we cook, we have color signals that allow us to make awesome meals. When we remove the pink from the sausage, that means it's done. That's it. No toxic masculinity. It's a phrase created to limit one's success. If you're more powerful than your neighbor, that's great. They may need you one day to help them if they're in trouble for listening to bad advice, made a mistake, or are just basically stupid. OK, let's make some hash browns.

Scrub the potatoes clean and grate them with a large-holed cheese grater. Put the grated potatoes in a colander and rinse them under cold water till the water runs clear. Drain the potatoes, and then place them potatoes on several paper towels. Remove as much moisture as you can. Rinsing the grated potatoes and drying them well also removes excess starch. Now don't get me wrong, we want starch. Starch is the most flippin' important carbohydrate our body uses for energy. Without energy, we are just sloth-like followers of an ideology that promotes collective failure, lack of individualism, and acceptance of weakness. When you hear or read some rhetoric that starch is bad, it's another chapter of nonsense that attempts to confuse the good Americans of this country to change, not only their diet, but a basic chemical necessity for their body and mind to grow. Put the grated potatoes in a bowl and toss it with the salt, garlic powder, and onion powder. In the cast-iron skillet, warm the extra-virgin olive oil over medium heat. Spread the potatoes over the skillet evenly and press them down with a wooden spatula. Let them cook for 2 minutes. Stir those potatoes up and press them down again. Cook for another 2 minutes. Repeat. Keep turning them over in sections till the potatoes are golden brown and crispy. Probably about 6 to 8 more minutes.

Meanwhile, line a plate with a couple of layers of paper towels. Transfer the hash browns to the lined plate for a few minutes to absorb excess oil. Throw in a dash of salt.

Now cook up your chopped onions for a few minutes. When done, put them in with the sausage. In a bowl, beat those eggs, then add milk, parsley, and salt and mix together. Put your potatoes in the skillet. Pour the egg mixture over them. Then quickly add the sausage and egg mixture. Cook and stir gently over medium heat till the eggs are set. Sprinkle your cheddar cheese on top. Cover for 1-2 minutes or till the cheese melts.

Presentation

You can nicely cut the display into quarters for sharing with family and friends or just set the cast-iron skillet on a pot holder and eat the whole damn thing yourself. Here's a fun idea: get three other people to share your delicious breakfast. Each of you sit at a cardinal direction on the table representing north, south, east, and west. Tell your favorite pro-American story about whatever section of the USA you represent. If you don't have anything positive to say about your region, open a history book and learn something. Every section of our great country has contributed and made a positive effect on the country we now know as the great United States of America. If you're eating right out of the skillet, be careful. It's hot.

Illegal waffles
I've never been particularly excited about this dish... I'll explain later

Ingredients

2 eggs
2 cups all-purpose flour
4 teaspoon baking powder
2 tablespoon sugar
1 teaspoon salt
1 and 1/2 cups whole milk from a cow
6 tablespoon unsalted butter from a cow, melted
1 teaspoon vanilla extract

Instructions

Preheat that waffle iron. Also, melt the butter in a pan on the stove. Definitely make sure it doesn't get brown. Another step… warm the milk in a pan on the stove. Now, your whole stove is basically occupied. Ridiculous. On your counter, pour the flour, sugar, baking powder, and salt in a large bowl. Whisk to combine. In a separate small bowl whisk the eggs and stir in the warm milk, melted butter, and vanilla extract.

In yet another bowl, mix everything together and whisk till blended. This is now the batter. Yay! Batter up! Now ladle the batter into the preheated waffle iron and cook till the waffles are golden brown and crisp. Hope you enjoy cleaning that waffle iron later on.

Presentation

Serve topped with any of a number of things and excitedly watch as they go into the cute little indentations. Don't they remind you of tiny safe spaces? You can use butter and maple syrup, fruit syrups, honey, or powdered sugar. Did you know that most people who suck say Belgian waffles are better than regular waffles? They even refer to our waffles as "denser and thinner with less texture." This is just a blatant lie. You know what? I'm getting ticked off. Just throw that stupid foreign-made waffle iron in the garbage... better yet, throw it in your illegal foreign neighbor's garbage if you have one. See, the better choice is the pancake. This is a delicious and more reasonable alternative to the goofy waffle, that needs some Chinese-made apparatus to cook the mixture. Pancakes need a flat pan and some heat. Simple. Affordable. Efficient. See, most waffle eaters are lonely people who usually eat breakfast alone. Very sad. Pancake eaters have big families, lots of friends, and eat breakfast with lots of people. Could you imagine trying to make one gosh damn waffle at a time for 8 screamin' youngins who are starving? Not feasible. Now, let's make some good ole American pancakes!

Colonial pancakes
(with cool alternate names like… hotcakes, griddlecakes, or flapjacks)

Ingredients

1/2 cup (1 stick) butter, melted and cooled
2 and 1/2 cups flour, spooned and leveled
1/4 cup white sugar or you can also add 3 tablespoons
dark brown sugar
1 teaspoon salt
2 teaspoons baking soda
2 tablespoons baking powder
2 cups buttermilk
1/2 cup whole milk from an American cow
2 eggs, separated
Bacon grease, for frying (butter works, too)
Maybe a teaspoon of vanilla

Instructions

Heat the oven to 170 degrees Fahrenheit or maybe it's a keep warm setting on newer models. Get yourself 3 bowls. A big one, a medium one, and a small one. Melt the butter and place in the large bowl. Add the buttermilk and milk in the same large bowl. Now, let's move on to the medium bowl. In the medium bowl, whisk together white flour, white sugar, white salt, white baking soda, and white baking powder. Time for the small bowl. Separate the eggs (if you don't know how to do this, call someone who does). Add the egg whites to the small bowl, and use a small whisk or fork to beat the egg whites a little bit. Only 20 seconds or so till they start getting a little bubbly. Add the yolks to the large bowl with the butter and milk. Whisk in the yolks. We're at a good point. The medium and small bowls are all white and are the foundation of our pancakes (unless you added brown sugar). The large bowl is yellow. Now we're going to have to mix them. It's time to fire up that griddle or large frying pan over medium heat with a little grease or butter.

Add the butter, milk, and yolk mixture to the ingredients in the medium bowl. Stir gently till all ingredients are combined. Grab the small bowl with the egg whites and add the whites to the medium bowl contents (you can add vanilla here… who doesn't like all things vanilla?). Fold in gently. Your batter is ready for cooking.

When the griddle is warm, scoop the batter using a half-cup measurement. Add the batter to the griddle from the center and gently pour in a circular movement going out to help the batter spread into a nice round circle. See, beginning at the center is an important aspect. When you start from the edges, it won't turn out. The center gets fat and the edges are too thinned out and will eventually get burned. See the analogy here. In this country, we start from the center and work our way out. The core is strong, but not too greedy, and the outside little people get their fair shake as they are evenly portioned with the center. What I'm saying is, for our country to work correctly, we have to start focusing on the center (the government) and make sure there is parity so that the outside portions (the working awesome Americans) don't get screwed. Communists countries are big on having a weak outside and a too powerful inside. Everyone there goes from the frying pan into the fryer. It's important to cook your pancakes slowly on medium heat. When you see bubbles forming on top, flip the pancakes. Be sure you shove that spatula all the way under. The pancakes should be a nice golden brown. Post-flip, continue cooking for another 2-3 minutes till they are golden on both sides. Transfer the pancakes to a cooking rack and keep warm in the oven that you turned on before. Repeat with the remaining batter.

Presentation

Pancakes are great any time of the day or whenever you feel like eating them. They make everyone's tummies happy. If you're stuck in the kitchen and serving a large group, doll out the pancakes in batches with a serving dish. You may miss the whole eating together at the table meal, but who cares. You're a hard-working unselfish American. You take pride in serving others. You take pride in making other people happy. You don't have to be waited on, take handouts, or have to be included in everything that every stinkin' other group does. Back to the presentation. Serve pancakes with a variety of wonderful toppings. Maple syrup, cinnamon, chocolate treats, fruity pieces, creamy or crunchy toppings, or I'm sure you can probably make some sort of booze sauce if you need that morning fix. I hope that's not the case. See, this country was founded on 13 tiny colonies kicking down the all-powerful UK back in the day. These folks controlled probably a quarter of the whole world. You know how they did it? They told the people and the troops that other places were in dire need of their help. These foreign people all over the globe were not self-sufficient and were unable to survive under the tyrannical powers that controlled them. Well guess what? England came in, defeated who was ever in charge, and then became the tyrannical power. They didn't free these colonies and countries throughout the globe. They trapped them. Well, I got news for you. This is happening right here in our beloved United States. The politicians who want to control everyone set it up like this: they'll send all the poor people to one section and promise them free hand-outs from the government. They say these needy people are incapable of living successfully on their own. Another lie. They cage these people in an area where there is no hope, no jobs, and shitty education. There aren't even grocery stores in these areas. They do the same damn thing the British did. "These sad people need our help. We will come to their rescue. Ssshhh... we'll get their votes every time, and all we have to do is throw them some cash and some food every once in a while. Oh, we're not going to give them any opportunity. That's out of the question. Why would we do that?" Hey assholes. Give the American people something to strive for. We see right through your mirage. I can't stand these greedy politicians and their evil ways. We are Americans. We are strong. We will succeed. Hope you find the pancakes tasty.

No nonsense oatmeal

For Americans

Ingredients

1 cup steel-cut oats; these are the least processed of all
the diversities of oats
1 cup whole milk
2 cups water
1/4 teaspoon salt
1/2 teaspoon ground cinnamon
2 teaspoons honey
Any well-selected and appropriate toppings

Instructions

Oatmeal is a type of coarse flour made of groats, the oat
kernel that has been removed from the husk. Steel-cut
oats are the best. They are toasted and cut oat groats.
They are sometimes called "Irish oatmeal," which isn't an
ideal name, but what the heck. The oats are left whole
and cut into pieces with a steel mill. Steel cut oats
maintain the best texture when cooked. And yes, they
take a lot longer to cook than quick-cooking oats, but
they're totally worth it. Steel-cut oatmeal is

simultaneously delicious, creamy, and superior to lesser forms of oats.

In a good-sized saucepan on the stovetop, bring 1 cup of whole milk, 2 cups of water, and a pinch of salt (if desired) to a boil in a small saucepan. Stir in 1 cup oats and reduce heat to low. Simmer for 20 minutes. Add the 1/2 teaspoon of ground cinnamon and 2 teaspoons of honey. After that, the oats will need anywhere from 5 to 10 minutes of additional simmering to reach the texture you prefer. Again, great oatmeal may take a little more time than those fake oats. Like that Tolstoy Russian jerk wrote that the greatest warriors are patience and time, or something like that. You know this guy was a Christian anarchist who had ideas that Christians were of an anarchy fundamental, because they only answer to God. This is the kind of just straight out lying crap that turns Americans against each other. Tell our great men and women of the military who have faith that they are anarchists of the USA! Tell your church-going neighbor they are anarchists of our country. You know what? I wish I never would have brought this dude up. Sure, his quote is pretty cool for oatmeal, but a warrior is out on the field, not in the frickin kitchen over the stove. God bless our troops! If you like your oats chewier, stop cooking them sooner. If you're missing some choppers, and like softer, thicker, and creamier oats, let them go the whole extra 10 minutes. Note: steel cut oats will continue to thicken as they cool. It won't take you long to master it. You're a true American. You get it.

Nonsense oatmeal

For non-Americans

Ingredients

1/2 cup rolled oats; better to simplify it for you as quick or instant oats

1 cup milk; you can use some form of nut milk if you suffer from a dairy disorder

1/4 teaspoon salt

1 tablespoon butter; you'll probably have to use some form of nut butter

Mix-ins, as desired

I'm sure you non-Americans will love the idea of this. You'll probably like fresh fruits, chia seeds, or some kind of weird nut butter, sugar in the tank, cocoa powder, and I'm sure at some point you'll try to put some type of hallucinogenic herb or chopped up prescription to help you get through your oh so hard day.

Instructions

Stovetop: Bring 1 cup milk and a pinch of salt to a boil in a small saucepan. Stir in 1/2 cup oats and reduce heat to medium. Stir occasionally for 5 minutes. Add more milk or water if you prefer a thinner oatmeal, which I'm sure you do. Thin is good for non-Americans. Thin-minded, narrow-minded, closed-minded, etc. Remove from the heat, cover and let stand for 2 to 3 minutes. Add in any mix-ins that you desire. Where are the microwave directions, you say? Whatever.

Presentation

Put it in a fucking bowl. Duh. This is a quick snack that many non-Americans really enjoy. They're big fans of frozen dinners, meals that come in boxes and jars, and any other pre-made dish that they don't have to do themselves. They won't even use boiled water. They just add some water or odd nut milk and put it in the microwave. No attention to detail. No cares about doing things the right way, which God forbid may take a little longer and use some effort. Pity. Who raised these people anyway? I'm sure you'll enjoy any of these breakfasts we've gone over. They're a great start to your day. I'm sure my fellow Americans have plenty to do today.

Chapter 2

Stocks and Soups

Stock up
It is wise to be prepared

Ingredients

6 pounds of animal bones cut into about 3-inch pieces
(Beef, pork, veal, chicken, duck, game, fish or shellfish
parts)
1 gallon cold water
2 cups diced onion
1 cup diced carrot
1 cup diced celery
8 oz tomato paste
2 bay leaves
1/2 teaspoon dried thyme
1/2 teaspoon peppercorns, crushed
3 garlic cloves, crushed
12 parsley stems

Instructions

Place bones and meat in a roasting pan, one layer deep.
Cook at 375 degrees F turning bones over to cook evenly.
After they have been cooked through, put bones in a
large stockpot. You can also throw other parts of the
animal in the stew. For the fish and seafood, throw in

heads, shells, claws, tails or whatever. I wonder if animal activists have a thing for shellfish. I never see any substantial stand against mussels or clams. Oh, that's right. They can be selective and target any group of animals they want. Pitiful group of protestors. Save the fat and juices from the roasting pan. Cook the onion, carrots, and celery in the roasting pan for 10-15 minutes, till slightly browned. Add tomato paste. If you don't add paste, it'll come out clearer, sometimes called white stock. Next, add water to the pot and bring it to a simmer. Add in bones and meat. Add bay leaves, thyme, garlic, and peppercorns. Lower the heat to low. Loosely cover with a lid and cook for 6-8 hours. Strain off the stock as you're cooking. At the end, discard bones and bay leaves. Cool. Store for the future.

Why do we make stock?

Stock is the base in all soup-like foods. We make our own to avoid poisoning our bodies with what the food industry provides us. How many toxic chemicals are in those boxes of stock that have expiration dates out to 2 or 3 years? Aren't we flooded enough with the processed options that we currently have? Shit, there is even baby "food" in jars of all types. Have you ever looked at the expiration date on these things? Uh, why don't you just smash up whatever food you're eating and give it to your babies? Why is that so hard? Trust me it works. Kids eat what you eat. Then they got all those bars and wrapped toxic treats for your toddler. What are in those things anyway? Have you ever tried them? They taste like a nuclear power plant. Watch out for it. Now, after the little ones have ingested their processed meals for the first 3 years of their lives, the kid's first grade teacher says the little tyke has attention deficit disorder! Wonder why? Fuck it. Drug the little bastard. They might be a little fidgety and the teacher may actually have to teach. Fuck it. Drug everybody. The teacher is stressed out. Anxiety drugs. Anti-depression drugs. Hell, drug the parents. Poor things have to actually go to work, pay bills, and take care of their families. They must be having an awful time with that. Dope everyone. Keep original thought down and weaken the mind. It's all propaganda designed to subdue Americans. Now, everyone feels like a failure and needs even more drugs to cope. You know what? Let's kick ass. The American people are awesome. I was reading something the other day on self-confidence. It was very enlightening. What we face is the criticism of ourselves from ourselves. It's true. This is a learned thing that is taught from the leftist professors, media, and information outlets. They get into your mind and make you think you are not as good as you really are. Look at yourself. What do you actually do poorly? Hardly anything for fuck's sake. It's all mind manipulation so you won't succeed. They'll keep you at a level where you just do your minimal daily thing and not stir up the reality that big government is taking advantage of you. Screw them. You are a highly capable talented human being. You're American for God's sake. Be your confident self. Be great. Let's make some soup.

Black and white bean soup

Ingredients

1 pound dried black beans
1 pound dried Ultra Great White Northern beans
2 tablespoon ~~olive oil~~ regular American vegetable oil
1 cup chopped white onion
1 garlic clove, sliced
2 teaspoon ground sage
1/2 teaspoon salt
1/2 teaspoon ground red pepper
2 boxes extra-salt chicken broth (If you're incapable of actually making your own, in which case you're probable not able to do a lot of things on your own. Thanks for putting the government in charge of your life! You set a great example for the rest of the country.)
1/2 cup chopped fresh parsley

Instructions

Let's get started: sort and wash the beans. Make sure you discard white beans that have any imperfections, marks, deformity, are too small, or smell funny. Imperfections in the black beans can be expected. Soak beans overnight in purified water in refrigerator. You can place black and white beans next to each other, but ensure they are in separate containers.

The next day, place all the beans in a large Dutch oven, since the Netherlands try their hardest to be as inclusive as possible for some reason. Add water to a depth of 2 inches above the beans. Bring to a boil, cover, then let the beans stand for 1 hour and see how that goes. Wait a second. What the hell is wrong with me using a fucking Dutch oven. Slow cooking in a regular US-made pot on a stove top would have worked just as well if not even better. Throw the Dutch oven in the garbage. When finished cooking, drain the water off the beans and place in an American-made bowl. Place oil in a regular stainless steel pot on the gosh damn stove over medium-high heat. Add onion and sliced garlic. Sauté (French fancy lingo for cooking in fat) for a few minutes. Add ground sage, red pepper, and broth.

Grab a soup spoon and taste a mixture of black and white beans. If the black and white beans are working together to help the greater good of the entire soup, that's what we want. If any beans are not contributing, remove them and immediately discard them in the garbage with that damn Dutch oven. We're working toward a soup that succeeds! We don't have time to use ingredients that are just taking away from the greatness of our meal. Cover the most wonderful blend of ingredients, reduce the heat, and simmer for about an hour and a half. Throw in some chopped parsley. Make sure you stir up the soup every ten minutes or so. You don't want the bottom of the mixture to burn. It'll ruin the whole thing. You've worked hard at this soup. Make sure you get the most out of it.

Presentation

Get your hard-working lovely God-fearing Grandma's ladle and finest bowls and enjoy the best damn soup you've had in a while. While you're enjoying the soup, here are some things not to do today: watch some fake news show and try to relate it to your own life, pretend to be a freedom fighter (those people actually save lives), take a picture with someone of another race to act like you are a worldly person, talk shit about the state of the Union, picket for causes you don't know jack shit about, don't be stupid if you can help it, don't ignore your neighborhood, don't ignore your family, don't ignore your friends, act like the police are against you, think that people in the military are anything but exemplary, think you know more than the person next to you, treat animals poorly, be selfish, refuse to be aware of your surroundings, underestimate people, undermine people, talk over people, forget to say thank you and you're welcome, knock down other people's creations, think you know everything, or be rude. The bean soup goes great with toast. You can dunk it or eat it on the side.

You got balls lentil soup

Ingredients

1 cup lentils
1 pound ground chuck
1 egg
1 cup tomato sauce
2 cups (also a quart) of water, not that bottled junk
2 cups beef stock or beef bouillon (That paste bouillon is actually pretty tasty, but you'll need 2 more cups of water, but I would highly suggest making your own damn stock. It's way better for you. You aren't going to shove a boat load of needless preservatives in your system.)
1 tablespoon vegetable oil
2 cloves garlic, minced
6 carrots thinly sliced
5 celery sticks thinly sliced
1 white onion thinly sliced
1 tablespoon butter from a cow
1 tablespoon grated parmesan cheese
1 tablespoon chopped fresh parsley
3 tablespoons bread crumbs
Dash of salt
Some ground black pepper

Instructions

Heat oven to 350 degrees. Meanwhile, heat a pot of 2 cups water and 2 cups of your beef stock on high. Let's get your balls ready. Combine ground chuck, the egg (without shell), some parsley, some garlic, parmesan cheese, and bread crumbs in a large bowl. Get your hands in there and mix that shit up. Start making little meatballs by taking a chunk of meat, roll in a small ball in the palm of your hands. Place each ball on a cooking sheet covered with aluminum or tin foil. Don't cover the meatballs, cover the sheet. You should have a nice little army of balls ready to go. Place the meatballs on the center rack in the oven. Your pot should be boiling by now. Once you bring the pot to a boil, reduce heat to low, add lentils, and cook 20 minutes. The meatballs need to cook for about 30 minutes.

Heat up a medium frying pan with butter. Get your sliced carrots, celery, white onions, and the rest of the garlic. Fry 'em up in the pan for about 10 minutes.

After the lentils have been simmering for 20 minutes, add the carrots, celery, white onions, and the rest of the garlic to the pot. Throw the tomato sauce in. Add the salt and pepper. Add any other spices you want. It's soup for goodness sake. Boom! Transfer the cooked meatballs to the pot. Return to a boil, reduce heat to medium-low, and simmer for 40 minutes.

Presentation

This is a hearty stand-alone soup. It's a meal packed with goodness. Did you know lentils grow up in pods like peas and beans and most followers of one political party in our country that wants to not only screw everything up, but wants to keep it jacked up? That's right, pods. People who live in pods are unaware and unprepared for what's out there. They create safe zones and safe places. Do they really think this helps anything? What it is, is a form of separation and segregation. Americans need to stick up for themselves. Do you think the real feminists had fucking safe zones? No. They fought. I know this woman, who went to college for accounting and a highly respected college in the early 1960s. Did she go on a silly talk show or have a stupid blog to tell everyone what she did? Heck no. She got great grades and then applied to all sorts of companies who required top-notch accountants. She was denied multiple times. Did she protest? Nope. She kept fighting. She's a proud American. She kept on with persistence and intelligence. Did she give up? Of course not. She finally was hired by a top-tier company. For decades, she worked her ass off. One day was married. Had kids. Prayed. Raised her kids in an educational church-going, God-fearing environment. Guess what? Her family is extremely successful, her career blossomed, and she retired with the respect of her entire field. Now she's enjoying as much time with her grandkids as she can. She's not concerned about her next vacation. She's concerned about life. This woman is a true inspiration. The so-called feminists of today disgust her. They want everything handed to them. They don't know what it "takes" to succeed. If they followed her, and many other women's leads, they would be successful and not just a bunch of lazy, think they know something, whining crack heads that only think about their own agenda and not the better good of everyone. When we each succeed, the group succeeds. A simple concept that those people just don't get. I really like this soup.

~~French~~ American onion soup

Ingredients

6 large red or sweet onions (about 3 pounds), peeled and
  thinly sliced root to stem
2 cloves garlic, minced
8 cups of beef stock
4 tablespoon olive oil
2 tablespoon butter
1 teaspoon sugar
1 teaspoon salt
1/2 teaspoon freshly ground black pepper
1 1/2 cups of grated ~~Swiss Gruyere~~ white American
cheese
1 tablespoon flour
1/2 cup dry red wine and 2 tablespoon brandy
2 sprigs thyme fresh, tied with kitchen twine
2 bay leaves
2 cups croutons

Instructions

Let's make some croutons. Don't be a lazy ass and
buy that processed crap with strange seasonings or
wheat bread or some other strange vegetable
crouton. Make it the right way. Get some bread that's

at least a day or two old. Any variety of white bread will work. Dice your bread with a knife so that the croutons will be equal sized so that they cook evenly. See, it's about equality, not favoritism. Don't use the crusts. Toss the bread with oil and any seasonings you like in a large bowl. Spread out the cubes on a parchment-covered baking sheet in a single layer. Bake till crispy by flipping the croutons once halfway through baking. Then baking till they croutons reach your desired level of crispiness. If they start to get too brown, lower the heat and let them bake lower and slower.

Time for soup. Onions can be grown from seeds, small dormant bulbs grown the year before, or transplants. All of these forms can grow well in almost any garden. Even transplant onions don't need a safe space to grow in. They only need to be planted about an inch below the top of the soil. Unlike our current situation, onion transplants require only about two months to reach maturity. Wouldn't that be nice? They get how to adapt to their environment and grow. Place onions in a medium sized ceramic bowl. Sprinkle with flour, pepper, and salt. In a medium stock pot, melt the butter then add the sliced onions. Toss onions in the butter till they are translucent. Add the sugar. Turn heat to low and cover. Cook till onions are caramelized (they'll be a slightly brown color). See, this was originally made by the warriors of the great ancient Greek and Roman civilizations. They just made onion soup. They didn't have to "caramelize" the onions like the French to make it sweet. They were tough. They didn't let any old dickhead into their country without kicking their ass. They took no shit from no one. The onion mixture will take about 45 minutes to cook. Move onions around frequently to ensure even cooking. Add the beef stock, wine, thyme, bay leaves, and garlic. Cook for about 30 minutes on low. Turn off heat. Stir and allow to sit for about 10 minutes. This will allow the cheese to cool a bit and all the goodness of the soup to get to a relatively good eating temperature.

Presentation

Portion the onion soup into oven safe bowls. Place a handful of delicious homemade croutons on top of the soup. Place cheese on top of the croutons. Place under the broiler till the cheese begins to bubble just a bit. Serve in those soup bowls and make sure you let company know that it's hot. Wouldn't want anyone to burn the roof of their mouth, even though I'm sure everyone at your dinner table has gosh damn health insurance. I wonder what health insurance is like in Afghanistan? Maybe they have blue rocket/blue bomb coverage or like a two-camel deductible. Sheep and women probably are part of the friggin barter system, too. Do they even have currency over there? Who gives a crap? In this country, everybody can get health insurance. Just pay for it. You know how expensive everything would be if we got free insurance for going to the doctor? It'd be insane. Oh, and guess what we also have. Yes. Real doctors and nurses. A lot of places around the world have medicine men who make all kinds of nasty potions that make people even sicker. And they get away with this. Not here! We have trained medical staff who actually care about you and help you get better. God bless our hard-working and dedicated healthcare and emergency medical teams in the U.S.A.!

Russian borscht soup

Ingredients

2 cups fresh beets
2 cups chopped carrots
2 cups chopped onion
4 cups beef or vegetable stock (When this soup is the only thing you're eating because the commies gave our country to Russia, none of us will be able to afford to eat any meat. So, when you make your stocks, save that lovely broth, because we'll all be broke and starving.)
1 can (16 ounces) diced tomatoes, undrained (You're gonna have to use canned foods once Russia takes over because the left ding dongs jacked up everything and just handed the country over because of their laziness and lack of vision)
2 cups chopped cabbage
1/2 teaspoon salt
1/4 teaspoon pepper
Sour cream
1/2 teaspoon dill weed

Instructions

Boil the beets for about 24 minutes. Taps has 24 notes. The hardest 24 notes a bugler can play. It's the song they play at military memorials and funerals. It'll be the death of our way if these communist politicians and blind followers have their way. So disrespectful. Set aside the beets. Peel and grate. In a large saucepan, combine the carrots, onion, and broth. Bring the mixture to a boil. Reduce heat, cover, and simmer for 30 minutes. Add tomatoes, beets, and cabbage then cover and simmer for 30 minutes or till cabbage is tender. Stir in salt, dill and pepper. Pretty basic.

Presentation

Top each serving with sour cream and dill. To get the most authentic experience, go down to the nearest homeless shelter and offer them some money for their old, dirty, smelly torn up clothes. The hell with it, bring the kids. The whole family can enjoy the experience. Walk home, turn off all the lights, the heat and air, TV, or anything electric, 'cause you're not gonna have any of the possessions we have in this great country. It'll be a shit show. Get out your candles, light them with a match. Now go to the basement or garage and grab anything that will work as a bowl. This is what you'll be eating out of the rest of your life. Oh, have you ever eaten soup with a wooden spoon? Fun, huh? Sit on the floor. Eat your damn communist soup and tell stories to your offspring about how life used to be when true Americans were the backbone of our beloved country. Now rip this page out of the cookbook and burn it. We are America. We are strong. We will never be taken over. When the soup is ladled into the bowls, let it cool for a few seconds and then add a scoop of sour cream. The sour cream really adds a nice tasty touch to this comrade soup. No Strovia, or however you say it.

Chapter 3

Lunch

Mayonnaise for stuff

Ingredients

3 eggs
1 teaspoon salt
White pepper
1 teaspoon Dijon mustard
3 tablespoon white wine vinegar
1 pint salad oil
Lemon juice, to taste

Instructions

Separate the highly nutritious egg yolks and put in the bowl of a mixer. That's right. Egg yolks are full of wonderful nutrients contrary to the fake news you've been hearing for years. The yolk, or yellow shit, contains all of the fat in the egg and a little less than half of the protein. So, don't eat egg yolks they say? Get ready for this. The yolk has just about all the vitamins, with higher proportion of vitamins B6, B12, and folic acid. All of the A, D, E, and K vitamins are found in the yolk. Yep, egg yolks are one of the few foods in the world that naturally have vitamin D. The yolk also contains more calcium, copper and iron, manganese, phosphorus, and zinc than the white part of the egg that the big government companies tell you to only eat.

Whip on high speed till frothy. Add a dash of salt and white pepper with one and a half tablespoons of white wine vinegar to the yolks. Whisk to combine. Now, add the salad oil one drop at a time till the mixture begins to thicken. Add the rest of the oil in a slow steady stream, thinning the mixture occasionally by adding a little vinegar. Continue till all the oil and vinegar have been incorporated. Add a squirt of lemon juice. Refrigerate.

Why we make our own mayonnaise?

Haven't you caught on to the theme yet? Do the work yourself. Don't leave it up to someone else. You're a hard-working American. The whole country rises and excels, because of people doing tasks for themselves. The country falls when you have other people take care of your business. Do you need historic events to show this to you? Get off your ass and get it done. You want a new car? Make enough money to buy one. Don't borrow money. Are you stupid? Uh, if I don't have a mortgage, I can't write it off on my taxes. Hey dumb-dumb, you're paying thousands of dollars in interest to get back a few hundred on your taxes. Don't listen to the government advice! It's holding you back. Seriously. Look at your tax return from last year. How much did you pay in interest, which is not invested back into your house, versus what you got back by having a silly "write off?" Don't count on the government to help you financially, emotionally, or physically. It's all bullshit. You're strong. You're more than capable. You're American. Mayonnaise goes great on almost any sandwich. Don't used that processed crap. And go to your local butcher for meat and cheese. Go to your local baker for bread. It may cost a little more, but who cares anyway? You're giving away thousands of dollars every year with your loans and credit cards. At least they were smart enough and work diligently to have a meat market or bakery. Also use fresh vegetables. Grow your own gosh damn garden. It's not that hard. Also, bring your lunch to work. Stop wasting money buying some crap or fast food. You know what's a good idea? Bring your own darn lunch to work. If you spend 6 dollars a day on lunch, that's 30 bucks a week. Times that by 50 weeks and now we're talking about 1500 dollars a year. For lunch. I brought my lunch to work and not only did I save money, but I was also eating healthier. I didn't have some salt and sugar-based meal from some crappy chain restaurant that could give two shits about your well-being. You are in charge of taking care of you, Period. If you want your sandwich nice and fresh after you've been at work your first 3-5 hours, before you go to work, wrap it in tin/aluminum foil. It'll keep it fresh. Trust me.

Thousand Island dressing for stuff

Ingredients

1 teaspoon red wine vinegar
1 teaspoon sugar
2 ounces mayonnaise
2 ounces ketchup
1 1/2 ounces sweet pickle relish
1 hard-boiled egg, chopped
1/2 tablespoon fresh parsley, chopped
3 green onions, chopped
Salt, dash
Pepper, dash
Worcestershire sauce, dash

Instructions

Combine vinegar and sugar. Stir till sugar is dissolved. Now add remaining ingredients: the mayo you made yourself, ketchup, relish, chopped egg, parsley, green onions and mix. A good hint to boil an egg is to put it on ice. It'll help when you peel the shell off. You know a lot of our great veterans have a problem with PTSD, which is combat-related post-traumatic stress disorder. After we kicked some ass in World War I, a lot of our heroes had what was called shell shock. This is PTSD. A real disorder that needs to be addressed and fixed. Not these fake disorders that the wusses we have to share our great country with come up with. The veterans need help. The whiners need to get a life. Add salt, pepper, and a dash of Worcestershire sauce. Refrigerate. Add to your favorite home-grown salad or sandwich.

Presentation

Thousand Island dressing is named after its origins on the group of islands that are part of our beautiful state of New York. Some of the islands are part of Canada, but of course, they had no part in the invention of this classic and tasty dressing. Thousand island dressing is great on all kinds of salads and even on sandwiches. Be careful though, this was a common Russian move as there is a Russia dressing that's similar to the lovely Thousand Island dressing that can be used on sandwiches. Thousand Island dressing, of course, has taken over as the leader in sandwich dressings, but there still may be those out there who enjoy the spicier Russian dressing. I bet their palate was developed by the spicy foods of Mexican, South American, or Asian cuisine. Be aware. Americans have excessively well-developed taste buds. We don't need spicy shit. We need food that's healthy and fresh. We do things that are good for us to build spirit and resilience.

Special lunch: ultra-leftist toss your salad

Bahahaha… go to the most expensive place you can find with a co-worker, hang out pal, or acquaintance and buy a special salad. You probably want to be seen somewhere popular. Now take your salad and shake it really good. Add your dressing. Shake it again. Now toss… toss… toss with your partner. That's what you do best. Next!

Balsamic and roasted garlic vinaigrette for stuff

Ingredients

8 cloves of garlic
1 ounce balsamic vinegar
3 ounces olive oil
1 teaspoon mustard Dijon
Salt
Pepper

Instructions

Roast the garlic at 350 degrees F in the oven till soft and golden brown. Peel the skin off and either smash it up really good or puree it. Whisk in the vinegar, Dijon mustard, and salt and pepper to the garlic. Whisk in the olive oil. Done.

Presentation

What the hell is balsamic anyway? This vinegar is not a wine vinegar, because it's not from fermented grapes. It's from this crap called must. Grape must is made up of the skins, seeds, and stems crushed and mixed together. So balsamic is like grape juice vinegar. The thing is, you have to age balsamic vinegar like wine. That's why it's so damn expensive. So, if you get a good bottle of balsamic vinegar, make this vinaigrette and put it on all your salads and sandwiches. Speaking of hell, have lunch with some of your pals from the satanic temple. These folks mean business. Now, you may have heard about the satan church that was established back in the 1960s, but the temple people basically took down the satan church and called their religion a falsehood. Watch out for these people. They talk a big talk on Christian privilege, oh here we go again with this, and protected those who can't protect themselves. Ha, what the crap is going on? Don't fall for another socialist scheme disguised as something else. I don't think these assholes even worship Satan. They worship themselves. Anyway, when they come over, freak the fuck out of them by having a sacrificial goat in the backyard, poor some of your vinaigrette over the goat, get out a cool Viking knife and watch how they scream and cower. Call their BS and throw them out of your house. Tell them to take the goat with them. They'd probably make great goat people, sitting up in the hills, pretending to be better than everyone else. Shame on them. Oh, you can mix this vinaigrette with your homemade mayonnaise for a fantastic sandwich dressing. The hell with Satan and all his fake followers who don't even follow him. Maybe say a prayer before lunch. It's getting rough out there with all these groups.

Chapter 4

Main Courses

Ribeye steaks and cheesy potatoes
Now we're talking!

Ingredients

The steaks
2 large bone-in ribeye steaks, cut 2 inches thick
Freshly ground pepper
Garlic powder

The cheesy potatoes
2 pounds russet potatoes
1/4 cup butter
1/4 cup all-purpose white flour
1 and 1/2 cups half & half from an actual cow
Salt & pepper
2 cups freshly shredded cheddar cheese – do it yourself;
make America grate again
Paprika
Freshly chopped chives

Instructions

The potatoes take longer so let's get them started first:
preheat your oven to 350 degrees F (we use Fahrenheit
degrees here, not that Celsius form of measurement) and

grease a 13"X9" (" means inches) glass baking pan with cooking spray. Boil water in a large stainless- steel pot. Clean off the potatoes, peel, and place them in the boiling water. Cook for about 22 minutes. Take the potatoes out of the water. While the potatoes are cooking, make the cheese sauce. Melt your butter in a medium-size saucepan over medium heat. Whisk the flour with some cold water in a separate dish till it is like a paste. Add flour paste to the butter, whisking constantly, till the flour turns a beautiful golden color, probably about 2 minutes. Stir in half & half and heat about 2 to 3 minutes till it's thick. Remove from heat and stir in shredded cheese. It'll melt in perfectly. Season with a little salt and pepper. Slice the potatoes and place a third of the potatoes overlapping in a single layer in the baking dish. Spoon in some of the cheese sauce on top of the potatoes. Repeat making three layers of potato slices and cheese sauce. Sprinkle with 1/4 cup shredded cheddar and a little paprika. Bake for 25 minutes.

Let's cook up some Grade 'A' American beef: put on your favorite red, white, and blue cookin' shirt and preheat your grill on high. Important note: do not use grill in bathtub! Extreme fire hazard. Always use your grill outside, stupid. Place your ribeye steaks on a ceramic plate. Sprinkle a bit of pepper and garlic on each steak. Rub that goodness in. Flip steaks and do the same on the other side. When the grill is hot, place steaks over direct heat for 4-5 minutes on each side for medium rare. If you need to use a meat thermometer to determine if you've cooked steaks the way you like them, here are the temperatures you're looking for: 120 degrees F=rare, 130=medium rare, 140=medium, 160=well done. Take steaks off. Put on a clean ceramic plate and cover with aluminum foil for 5-7 minutes. Clean the grill right away. Don't be a lazy dirtbag.

Presentation

Bone appetite. Try to time everything so they're done at the same time. Take out the cheesy potatoes and garnish with the freshly chopped chives. Uncover those steaks. Always place the steak on the right side of the plate and the potatoes on the left. When setting out silverware, the forks go on the left and knives and spoons go on the right. Here's how this works. When you are in a situation where you are surrounded with a bunch of elitist left-headed fakers who think they're something and try to fancy up everything, there may be a bunch of silverware surrounding your plate. They're going to want to see you fail or ask which utensil to use first. It's simple. Start on the outside and work your way in. So, first course would be the outermost fork on the left or spoon on the right. Also, make note that the knife should have the blade side in toward the plate. Then as each course continues, use the next piece of silverware going in. See, you're a well-mannered and etiquette knowledgeable American. You know what? You're better off with your real friends at home. Hey, if you need to pick up that bone and gnaw the rest of the meat off it, do it. If your company has a problem with that, throw them out of your house. Fuck 'em… you're a true American.

Take your time pot roast and green beans

Ingredients

2 pounds beautiful cheap beef
   Your choices: chuck (chuck roast, shoulder steak, boneless chuck roast), brisket, or round
1 red onion
1 pound mushrooms of your choice
4 cloves garlic
1 cup beef stock
Pepper
Vegetable oil
3 teaspoons butter
1 pound green beans, trimmed (make sure they are dry and fresh)
5 cups water
Worcestershire sauce (seriously, who knows how to pronounce or spell this?)

Instructions

Get out grandma's iron skillet and fire that sucker up on high on the stove. After a bit, put in some vegetable oil. Take your pot roast meat and pepper it on all sides.

When the skillet is pipin' hot, put the meat in there. Sear that beautiful piece of cow on all sides. At the end, take out the roast and set aside, toss in the red onion and mushrooms (sliced medium size), add some Worcestershire sauce, and just fry up a little. Set aside.

Oven cooking: Turn oven on to 175 degrees. Place roast in a large baking pan with 2 cups water or beef stock. Add in onions, mushrooms, and remaining juices and sauce from cast iron skillet. Cover pan with aluminum foil.

Crock pot cooking. Turn crock pot on low. Place roast in with 1 cup of beef stock. Add in onions, mushrooms, and remaining juices and sauce from cast iron skillet. See, I don't put carrots and potatoes and all those other flavors in my pot roast. That would be a stew and should be under soups, not gosh damn main courses. Back to cooking… so, you're gonna have 10 hours to kill. Any regular hard-working American would go to work. If you don't work, at least get something done for the day. Go to the laundromat. It's the only place left in America where you can separate the coloreds and the whites and not have everyone freak out about it.

When you get back home, or wherever you're cooking, place 2 cups of water in a pan and bring to a boil. Add the cut green beans and a pat of butter and reduce to medium heat. Cook till your desired crispness. Probably about 15 minutes. After you start the beans, take out the roast, put it on a platter and cover with foil. Let it set for a while and that thing will be an awesome American piece of delicious and tasty and juicy beef.

Presentation

Oh ya! Slice up that roast, put it on a plate, cover it with sauce, mushrooms, and red onions, put those lovely green beans next to it, and enjoy. Drink whatever the heck you want with it. Did you see that propaganda about how eating beef causes global warming? Yes. From cows farting. Our beautiful American cows all over our beautiful country are being accused of causing harmful gas distribution in the atmosphere, because they're sitting peacefully on the farm, just waiting their turn to be someone's delicious breakfast, lunch, or dinner, and they're farting so much that the world is now in a state of global warming. That's right you coward, blame the stinkin' cow. Don't look at all the energy you use to make your life nice and easy. Every douche bag walking around taking selfies all day, buying 5-dollar coffees in paper cups, eating out lunch wrapped in nature-disabling packages, watching hours upon hours of television, using electricity for every little thing they do, I could go on and on. Stop blaming the poor cows. Speaking of crock pots… that, my friend, is a crock of shit!

Rosemary's baby chicken

Ingredients

1 whole chicken
1/2 cup butter
1/2 cup melted butter
1 cup chicken broth you were taught how to make
earlier
2 cloves garlic, minced
2 sprigs fresh rosemary (Yes, a sprig is a single stem of
   a fresh herb that's about 4 inches long or so. I just
   wanted to throw you off a bit.)
2 sprigs fresh thyme
2 sprigs fresh sage

Instructions

Preheat oven to 350 degrees F. Pour the chicken broth into a small roasting pan, and set aside.

Loosen the skin from the breasts and thighs of the chicken. Shove pieces of butter underneath the skin of the chicken. This isn't particularly easy to do so take your time. Place chicken into the roasting pan. Tie up the legs together with kitchen twine (I'm sure you have an idea how to do this). Sprinkle the chicken with salt and pepper, then rub in the minced garlic all over the chicken. Drizzle the melted butter on top, then lay the herb sprigs onto the breast and around the legs. Cover with aluminum foil and bake for 20 minutes.

Now uncover and baste the chicken with the pan juices. Continue cooking till the chicken is no longer pink, or when a meat thermometer inserted into the thickest part of the thigh reads 165 degrees F, probably 1 to 2 hours. Baste the chicken every 10 to 15 minutes after you uncover it. Once cooked, allow the chicken to rest out of the oven for 10 minutes before slicing.

Presentation

Cut out the chicken breasts and legs first. Then separate them. Do the same for the thighs and legs. See the chicken parts work together in harmony. The white meat has a set of functions and the dark meat has another set of functions. Then they combine their functions to enable the whole chicken to work as one unit. See, the alt-left doesn't understand this. People are different. It's not only OK, it creates perspectives in our country. I'm not saying anti-American perspectives, I'm saying creative, mathematical, and civically structural perspectives that allow us to improve our country. The alt-left wants to completely shut that system down. Shame on them. America as one. Not me as one against America.

Furthermore, those crazy leftist freaks will probably want to make this chicken, since they have no idea how to make fried chicken, because they never met or befriended anyone from the South or any in poverty or someone who actually works, I mean physically works, not just goes to a job, all day for a living.

Fiesta chicken fajitas

Ingredients

Not gonna happen.

Instructions

What is wrong with you?

The best country (in the world) fried chicken

Ingredients

1/2 cup milk
1 large egg
1 1/4 cups all-purpose flour
2 teaspoons salt
2 teaspoons ground black pepper
3/4 teaspoon poultry seasoning of a mixture of sage,
    thyme, marjoram, rosemary, and nutmeg
1 (2 and 1/2 to 3 lbs.) broiler-fryer chicken, cut up
1 cup all-vegetable shortening

Instructions

Combine milk and egg in a small bowl and beat with fork till frothy. Mix some of the flour, salt, pepper, and poultry seasoning in a resealable plastic bag. Shove that chicken in the bag like those sheep fuckers like to kidnap our good Americans and show them on those weird TV videos with some assholes covering their faces. Now shake that chicken really good. Dip into milk mixture. Shake chicken a second time in flour till it's coated. Now heat the shortening in either an electric or large heavy straight-sided frying pan till it reaches a temperature of 365 degrees F. Fry chicken uncovered till brown on bottom. That'll take about 10 to 15 minutes. Reduce the heat to medium-low and turn chicken over. Cover and fry 15 minutes. Uncover and continue frying 5 to 10 minutes till chicken is crisp and an inserted thermometer reads 165 degrees F.

Presentation

You'll never have to buy the combo meal again. Make some mashed potatoes and coleslaw and boom! Your family's gonna love you. Now this recipe is basic, but if you want some real American fried chicken, you're gonna have to go to the beautiful Southern United States. For some reason, these people got their fried chicken going on! They're fantastic. Fantastic people, with fantastic chicken. So be a regular American and go spend some time in the South. Not a gosh damn amusement park. The real South. Talk to people. Make friends. Don't be an ass. Go to a party. Have you ever been to a full-blown bash in someone's garage? It's awesome. I was at a bonfire one time that was two-stories tall. Kids were throwing aerosol cans in the fire because we ran out of fireworks. Dangerous? Not really. You'll be fine. Oh, and these folks seriously had a jousting tournament from the back of their pick-up trucks. Who in the hell has a working joust? You know who? Americans do. It was the best. Have the time of your life. Real Americans are beautiful people.

Stars and stripes lamb chops with herb butter

Ingredients

3 1-inch thick lamb chops
1 tablespoon oil
16 tablespoons unsalted butter, room temperature
7 garlic cloves
1.5 teaspoons fresh rosemary, finely chopped
Koshering salt, pinch
Salt
Pepper

Instructions

Roast the garlic at 350 degrees F in the oven. Peel and smash. Add the butter, garlic, rosemary, and koshering salt in a bowl. Whisk till butter is soft. Now turn over butter mixture with a wooden spoon till all ingredients are consistent throughout the butter. Cool.

Preheat the grill for 15 minutes on high. Season lamb chops with salt and pepper, brush with some oil. Oh, you can do this with veal, too. But wait. How horrible eating veal, because it's a baby cow. Well go fuck me, because lamb is a gosh damn baby sheep. No one pickets for that, do they? That's right, lamb is sheep. The Greeks love this kind of meat. They cook sheep with almost anything and anyway. They also make that gyro stuff which is basically a mixture of crappy meat compressed on that spicket thing. Screw that, give me a good old-fashioned American hotdog over that gyro drivel anytime. And what's with that cucumber sauce stuff? It doesn't even taste like cucumber. How about tomatoes, onions, pickles/relish, condiments on an awesome boiled or grilled hotdog and done. And what is that pita thing? Some kind of Mediterranean Middle East abuse of flour? I don't eat flatbread. I eat bread. Place lamb chops on grill. After 3-4 minutes turn. Grill another 3 or 4 minutes. Remove from grill, and let chops set for a few minutes.

Presentation

Sit at a round table and dress up like your favorite Greek god. Go for the whole experience and have you and your sibling dress up like Zeus and Hera. You know they were brother and sister, right? Imagine that. A whole religion based on the selfish and incestual actions of the lead gods in the whole thing. I think most of the Greeks have abandoned their pagan ways, but history does repeat itself. Let's just stick to going to church on Sunday. I like to put the butter in little lamb molds when

I cool them. Then you can put a little lamb butter slab right on top of the lamb chop. Yummy! That rosemary butter will melt right into your lamb chop.

Midwest fish boil

Ingredients

The main part
Four 1/2-pound whitefish steaks
1 and 1/2 pounds medium red potatoes
8 small white onions
2 tablespoons vegetable oil
2 tablespoons Kosher salt
2 tablespoons finely chopped fresh flat-leaf parsley
Freshly ground pepper
Melted unsalted butter and lemon wedges (for serving)

Tartar sauce
1 pint mayonnaise
2 ounces capers, chopped
3 ounces cornichon (those tiny pickles)
2 tablespoons onion, minced
2 tablespoons fresh parsley, minced
1 tablespoon lemon juice
Worcestershire and tabasco sauce

Instructions

Stir together all the ingredients for the tartar sauce. Chill.
See how easy that was?

Scrub the red potatoes to get all the dirt off. Potatoes grow in the ground. They're grounded. Like true Americans. Peel the onions. In a large stockpot, combine the potatoes and onions and add about 2 quarts of water covering the vegetables by 2 inches. Stir in 2 tablespoons Kosher salt and bring to a boil with high heat. Kosher salt. Hmm. Kosher. Well, as a matter of fact, Kosher salt is not like the foods of the vastly complicated Kosher dietary laws. Have you ever seen these? They're ridiculous. Those chosen people can hardly go out to eat and order anything. They have to have like 2 kitchens and 2 coolers, and 2 sinks, and it goes on and on. The salt is actually called Koshering. It's used to Kosher foods. The Kosher salt you see at the store is named to confuse you into thinking it's something special. It's not. Kosher salt is about the size. It's like sea salt. Table salt is very dense and used for baking and seasoning solid dishes. Kosher and sea salts are large and are a good source of salting for boils. Partially cover the pot and cook till the potatoes are not hard, about 15 minutes. Get your beautiful whitefish steaks and cook in a bit of oil to just slightly brown. Only a minute on each side. Now, arrange the whitefish steaks in a single layer on top of the vegetables. Partially cover the pot again, lower the heat to medium and cook till the whitefish flakes easily, about 10 minutes longer. Maybe we should call the highly sensitive lefties fish flakes instead of snowflakes? Did you see the fish flakes at the fun Midwest boil last Friday night? They kept asking for broiled fish, wanted to know if was farm-raised fish, had to sit far enough from the boil to make sure their kids didn't catch on fire, washed off the picnic bench with bleach wipes, and then popped a pill in each of their toddlers' mouths before they ate. They didn't bring any toys or something entertaining to read for the little ones and let them run all over the place bugging every adult in the area. Fish boils are awesome for true Americans. Non-selfish people who love to get together for simple and fantastic meals.

Presentation

Using a slotted big spoon, take out the whitefish and put on a warm platter. Put the potatoes and onions around the fish for a beautiful display of American brilliance. Fish boils originally were used to feed large groups of lumberjacks and fishermen. When's the last time you saw a real lumberjack? Not just some punk. with ignorant ideals. who was wearing skinny jeans (Uh, hello… lumberjacks don't wear skinny anything. They have lots of muscles from doing lots of work, so their clothes may appear a touch tight), a flannel shirt, and actually had on work boots. Ha! What a joke! Put a few lemon wedges on top. Sprinkle with parsley and pepper. On the side, serve the fish dish with cute little dipping cups (I have a set of very cool red, white, and blue ones) of melted unsalted butter and your homemade tartar sauce that everyone's gonna love. Successful fish boil achieved!

Southern USA shrimp and grits

Ingredients

1 cup stone-ground grits
3 cups water
2 teaspoons salt
2 cups half-and-half
2 pounds uncooked shrimp, peeled and deveined
1 pinch cayenne pepper
1 lemon, juiced
5 slices bacon
1 green, 1 red, and 1 yellow bell pepper, chopped
1 cup chopped onion
1 teaspoon minced garlic
1/4 cup butter
1/4 cup all-purpose flour
1 cup chicken broth
1 tablespoon Worcestershire sauce
1 cup shredded sharp cheddar cheese

Instructions

Bring water, stone-ground grits, and salt to a boil in a heavy saucepan with a lid. Yes. These are the real grits. Stone-ground grits are made from whole dried corn kernels. These kernels have been coarsely ground between the two stones of a grist mill. Stone-ground grits are less processed than the counterfeit counter parts: quick, regular, and instant. Stir in half-and-half and simmer till grits are thickened and tender, probably 40-45 minutes. The most important thing is to use a whisk and whisk often for smooth and creamy grits. And, yes, grits are from the great ole USA. In fact, they're a major dish in the Southern United States. This does not include the states by Mexico. Southern people are awesome and know how to keep their moral integrity. That's why they would never stoop so low s to use instant grits.

Now, sprinkle shrimp with salt, cayenne pepper, and a little lemon juice in a bowl. In the meantime, cook the bacon on a cooking sheet lined with aluminum foil at 350 degrees F for about 15 minutes in the oven. Keep the drippings on the side and put the bacon on paper towels. Get out a skillet, add some oil and the bacon drippings. Cook the green, red, and yellow peppers, onion, and garlic for about 7 minutes. Red, white, and blue peppers would totally be kick ass. I've never seen white or blue ones, but they exist.

In another saucepan, melt butter over medium heat. Stir in the flour to make a smooth paste. Turn heat to low and cook, constantly stirring till it's medium brown in color, about 8 to 10 minutes. Pour the butter-flour mixture into the skillet with the vegetables. Add in the shrimp. If you like to quickly woof down your shrimp dinners, don't want to eat the crunchy tails (which you can), and hate taking off the tails with each bite as you're enjoying your delicious Southern dish, slide off the tails from the shrimp before you cook them. Place the skillet over medium heat and pour in chicken broth, bacon that you previously cut up into little pieces, and Worcestershire sauce. Cook till the shrimp become bright pink. Only a few minutes. Don't overcook the shrimp. It'll be all rubbery and feel like you're chewing on a fat rubber band without any of the delicious shellfish taste when you cook these beautiful little shrimpies the right way and not too long.

Presentation

Just before serving, mix the cheese into grits till melted. Serve shrimp and veggie mixture over cheese grits. This is a beautiful dish that all of your Southern pals will love. They'll appreciate the meal. Have a blast. Get out your gun collection and tell them to bring their guns, too. For some real fun, you can use some cheap dishes and have a skeet shooting contest when you're done with dinner. Just have one of your guests hoist themselves on the roof, fling those plates as high as they can, and blast away! Great time had by all! Don't let the liberallies find out about it. They ruin everything. They'll probably try to ban grits on account of you and your guests "slaying and abusing" platters and having a good wholesome time. They silly, aren't they? Sometimes I try to look around a room and assess the people who are in proximity. I use a pretty complicated system for judging. 1) Would they have contributed during World War II? 2) Would they have survived World War II? Try it sometime. It's a great way to judge who your friends are and who your friends should be. Enjoy these great American dinners. Let's look at some other places around the world that may not have the opportunities we have. Living outside the United States is sub-American, but then again, there's the saying that some make excuses to fail and some make excuses to succeed.

Chapter 5

Foods From Our
WWII Enemies

Italian calzone (basically chicken pot pie with pizza type food in it)

Ingredients

Dough
1 packet of yeast
350 mL lukewarm water
950 mL flour
1 teaspoon salt
60 mL shortening

Filling
0.7 kg Italian sausage
0.9 kg ricotta cheese
7 eggs
120 mL grated romano cheese
120 mL minced parsley
Salt and pepper

Instructions

The European Union uses this metric system for measuring. Weighing in at about 2 pounds is the kilogram (kg), a unit of mass/weight. To fill your glass half full, you're gonna want about 200 milliliters (mL), a unit of volume. C is Celsius for temperature. Freezing is zero degrees C. Water that's boiling is 100 degrees C. Forget that. I'll take our American system any day! Dissolve the yeast in warm water. In a separate bowl, "cut" the shortening into flour and salt with a fork till there are no clumps. Add the yeast mixture. Make a dough ball and then knead for about 10 minutes. Put in a large bowl, cover with wax paper and a towel, and put bowl in a warm area. Let it rise for about 2 hours. Watch your favorite mob movie or go in the backyard and play that Bocci (I don't know how to spell it) ball game with the large red and green wooden balls and the tiny yellow ball. The best part is, when you don't cut your grass you can't see the tiny ball. Jarts would be way better. That's a game where you put down a circle about a foot and a half in diameter. You have these dart-like things that are about a foot long. They're weighted on the point end so that they stick in the ground. You launch one of these suckers about 15 feet in the air at a 45-degree angle. The circle is about 20-25 feet away so it takes quite a bit of skill. Guess what? The liberators of our great nation screwed that up, too. Oh, it's such a dangerous game for picnics and warm-weather outings. Ban it. The kids will get an oversized dart in the head. Ban it. Are you kidding me? We played this thousands of times. A little hint… don't let the damn kids go near the Jart game. Simple. Watch your kids. It's always better to hurt someone's feelings than a large dart in the head. Who likes sausage?

Italian sausage is basically pork sausage with fennel and garlic. Cut it into 1-cm pieces and brown in a pan. Drain off grease and set sausage aside to cool. I usually cool it overnight in the fridge. Preheat oven to 177 degrees C. Mix together cheese, 6 eggs, parsley, salt, and pepper. Add cooled sausage. Roll half the dough out and place in a 38 cm x 28 cm ungreased pan and fold over the sides. Spread in sausage mixture. Roll out the rest of the dough and place it on top. Pinch the edges kind of like a pie. Beat 1 egg yolk and lightly brush the top. Poke holes in the top with a fork. Bake for about an hour.

Presentation

During World War II the Italian people had this fascist leader who led them to their death by following Germany. Not sure what that was all about. Anyway, in the end after his assassination, the people strung that asshole up on public display. Read about this Mussolini guy. Scary shit. When he got in charge, he dissolved democracy. Then he removed all political opposition with secret police and outlawed labor strikes. He even made a series of laws that transformed the nation into a dictatorship. Within five years, he had established dictatorial authority by both legal and public-suppressing means and aspired to create totalitarian state. So, take note of the agenda of our socialist seekers. Meanwhile, back in the states, the Italian-Americans busted their ass for the great USA in the victory of World War II. They didn't defy America. They were appreciative of America. They were smart enough to realize that this is the greatest country in the world. Now cut and serve that calzone in sections for your family and friends. Talk about what fascism can lead to and how a European group assimilated to our great country.

Italian bruschetta

Ingredients

8 Roma tomatoes, diced
79 mL chopped fresh basil
60 mL shredded Parmesan cheese
2 cloves garlic, minced
1 tablespoon balsamic vinegar
1 teaspoon olive oil
Koshering salt, dash
1 loaf Italian bread (try to get a thin one)

Instructions

Let's toast the bread. Cut the bread about 1 cm thick. Place on a cooking sheet in an oven at 177 degrees Celsius for about 12 minutes. Brush a little oil on the bread before toasting. This is what makes bruschetta. It's not the toppings. You can put anything on top. Even smashed avocados. Yes! You can make avocado bruschetta that is even better than the infamous avocado toast that sells for 19 bucks a plate. Yep, they link the whole financial responsibility failure of the millennial generation to avocado toast. How about the government charging these damn kids two hundred thousand dollars to go to college? Shit, most of these kids don't even get degrees with any hands-on skills. Why do you need a degree from a university to sell crap? If you're good at it, just be a sales person. Communications major? Please. For what? So, these kids can be in huge debt at the start of their careers. How about four hundred thousand for a house? Ridiculous. Anyway, rub the balsamic vinegar and fresh minced garlic on the toasted bread. Now you have bruschetta. In a bowl, toss together the tomatoes, basil, cheese, and garlic. Mix in the olive oil, salt, and pepper. Sprinkle in some balsamic vinegar. Just a little.

Presentation

Serve the tomato mixture on the toasted bread slices. Your guests are going to love this appetizer right from the hearts of someone's grandmothers across Italy. Sit around enjoying the delight while mildly bragging to your well in-debt fake country club friends how you don't have a mortgage or car payment, because you know how to make your own bruschetta and not waste money on frivolous luxuries. They may be taken back a bit, but they really don't care. Too selfish. It's all about perception to them. They don't care what you're doing. They care about driving their fancy full-size SUV to the fanciest restaurants at 8 pm on Saturday night so they can be seen. Silly. You have value, not fake news clout. Give 'em some of your homemade wine and really get them going. They sputter so much repeated, self-contradictory statements and opinions that you'll be laughing about it for days. Sure, you'll be confused, because their logic is not logical. You'll enjoy it. Your guests will never forget the bruschetta time you had together.

German sauerbraten

Ingredients

1 kg horse
2 medium carrots, 2 medium sticks of celery
2 medium leeks
1 handful parsley, finely chopped
1 onion, finely chopped
2 bay leaves
10 juniper berries, 5 allspice berries (pimento berries)
5 black pepper corns
200 seeded raisins
2 granny smith apples, peeled and cut into cubes
250 ml sour cream
100 ml oyster sauce
Ground black pepper, dash
Olive oil for frying
300 ml light red wine
200 ml of red wine vinegar
200 ml dark port
500 ml pure water

Instructions

Make the marinade from the red wine, the red vinegar, and the water. bay leaves, juniper berries, pepper, and allspice. Allspice is not a mixture of spices, it's a berry from Jamaican. Bet the Nazis wouldn't be too happy about that. Boil the mixture and let it simmer for about 2 minutes. Let it cool down completely.

You're gonna need some horse meat. Let's see. You can always steal one from the closest race track. Maybe your gambling pals have some insider tips. But, be careful. Stealing a horse is a felony crime. Like stealing a car. Maybe you should just try to buy one. Not sure about that either. Some of those animal rights people are nuts. Place the meat carefully inside a sealed bag and pour the marinade into the bag. Put it in the fridge for two days.

After two days remove the horse from the marinade, season with salt and pepper. That horsey should be good and tender. Now, fry your four-legged friend in a hot saucepan in olive oil and oyster sauce. Russians loved killing everything close to them during World War II. I'm sure the poor and deprived people of Russia weren't for it, but Stalin didn't give two shits. Their psychopathic leader even murdered millions of his own people. And people in this country come out as pro-communist. Sick. Turn the heat down and add carrots, onion, leeks, celery, and fry for about 10 minutes. Pour the marinade into a bigger pan and add the parsley. Braise it in the oven for 2 and 1/2 hours at 190 Celsius. Stir occasionally so the meat doesn't burn. Add the apples and the raisins to the saucepan containing the liquid and cook for a further 10 minutes. Toward the end, stir in the sour cream. The

Russians are always putting sour cream in their foods. It makes me a little curious. Thank God I'm not a paranoid person.

Presentation

Remove the meat and slice 1 cm thick. Put the beautiful horse meat onto a serving dish. Pour that sauerbraten mixture over the meat. Notice that all of these countries have crappy meat. In the USA, you want a T-bone, all you have to do is walk down to the butcher or the grocery store and buy one. You don't have to marinade it for 2 days, cook it on low for a half a day, and serve it with a bunch of weird sauces and creams. Just put the steak on your American-made grill and cook it. Put a potato or corn on the cob on the grill, too. Kablamo! Meal served. American bellies are filled and happy. Ya. The pursuit of happiness. It's in the Constitution. The US Constitution. It doesn't read happiness. It reads pursuit. You've got to pursue it. That's right. You have to work at it. Fucked-up people in our country think they should be automatically given happiness. No, dumb ass. You have to make a plan, put some gosh damn effort into it, and go after it. Then, you'll be happy. Pay your bills. Do your job. Don't take short cuts. You think the great people who founded our country didn't have a plan and work their asses off? What the prick? You think our great men and women of World War II didn't pursue their plan? Fuckin' A right they did. God forbid you should have a job AND come home and cut your own lawn. Oh, I'm so exhausted, I'm gonna get some foreigner to clean my house. Stop being such a wuss or you're gonna end up like that horse... braised in some asshole's oven. OK. Let's eat some German food.

German sauerkraut

Ingredients

1 head cabbage, shredded
2 tsp koshering salt
1 teaspoons caraway seeds

Instructions

In a large bowl, mix the shredded cabbage with the salt and caraway seeds. Let the mixture sit for 20 minutes. Get a mason jar and pack the salted cabbage mixture into the jar. What's with this whole Freemason political subgroup of secrecy? I hear about it, but I never really see anything real about it. They say a bunch of our founding fathers were Freemasons, but what the hell does that mean? Are they trying to put a negative spin on their accomplishments? In fact, I'm not sure if the Freemasons are good or bad. It's always confusing on how the media presents their identity. I know some real masons. They lay brick, work with mortar, they set the stones. They build our great and long-standing structures of America. Pound the cabbage with a wooden spoon to pack it tightly and remove any air pockets. The cabbage should be submerged in salt juices. Get a storage bag and fill it with water. Seal the bag. This will act as a weight and keep the cabbage submerged. Cover the jar with a towel. Put the jar somewhere out of the way, away from direct sunlight, to ferment. Ferment for 1 week. When it's fermenting, it will start bubbling. If scum forms on the surface, just remove it with a spoon. Taste your sauerkraut every few days, and keep fermenting till you like the flavor. Take out the bag of water and cover the jar with an airtight lid. Store the sauerkraut in the refrigerator.

Presentation

Fry up an onion in butter. When the onions are nice and opaque, add some great German sausages. Let that sizzle for a while. When the sausages are almost done, add the sauerkraut and fry up for a few minutes, covered. Serve it with some good strong beer and everyone will love it. Though we consider sauerkraut a German thing, I'm sure it started in China or somewhere like that. Ya, the Germans are good people, but got all messed up by that socialist maniac bastard who started World War II. What a scum bag. If the intentions of our great Americans are not unadulterated, we may create a monster like Hitler here someday. Could you imagine that? Well you better stand strong now. Our American values are being threatened each day. No crazy dictators are welcomed here. What do we need in order to succeed? You. You Americans. You Americans continuing to be great and to keep progressing and accomplishing great accomplishments. Way to go my American friends. You are the best. I couldn't be prouder of the greatest country and people of the United States of America.

Japanese tofu

Ingredients

355 mL dried soy beans
1 L water
1 and 1/2 teaspoons nigari crystals or gypsum (the
   coagulants)
118 mL filtered or spring water

Instructions

Put the dried soybeans in the 1 L of water to soak
overnight. After soaking, transfer the beans and soaking
water to a food processor. Grind that mixture till the
liquid is smooth. That Emperor Hirohito basically wiped
out all of the Pacific Islands during World War II. These
Axis leaders in the Second World War were real mass
murderers. Japan ruled tons of people. Thank God we
got there. Our Marines were the toughest in the Pacific.
That's where the dirty fighting took place. But they
didn't complain about their rights and freedoms. They
fought for rights and freedoms. Our rights and
freedoms. Real Americans fighting a real enemy. In a
medium-sized pot, heat the soy slurry, uncovered, on
medium-high till it reaches a gentle simmer. Stirring
frequently with a wooden spatula. Use a strainer to

remove solids or any skin that forms on the surface. On the side, combine the nigari crystals or gypsum with filtered or spring water, and stir to dissolve.

Here's the fun part... put cookie cutters (these are our tofu molds) of your choice on top of a rimmed baking sheet, and arrange some liner cloth inside, letting its edges drape over the sides of the mold. When the soy milk is hot take it off the heat and let it sit for 2–3 minutes. Add the coagulant in three phases. Stir a wooden spatula in the mixture to get it moving. Pour in one third of the dissolved coagulant. Once the soy slurry stops moving, gently sprinkle in another third of the coagulant mixture into the slurry. Cover the pot and wait for three minutes. Sprinkle the remaining coagulant onto the surface. Now, gently stroke the wooden spatula back and forth across the topmost 1.25 cm layer for about 22 seconds. Now you'll see white curds in yellow liquid, Remove some of the yellow liquid from the pot. See, you want to keep the white stuff and remove the yellow. Just like the cowardly California, Oregon, and Washington politicians, and a Democratic President, who locked up Americans who were of Asian descent during World War II. Hey dumbasses, our fight was with Japan, not our fellow Americans. Do you know they locked up these poor bastards in camps underneath the highways? Oh, they won't talk about that, will they? I'm talking about American citizens! Ladle a touch of the yellow liquid into your tofu mold to moisten the liner cloth. Now ladle the curds into the mold. I like to use cookie cutouts of my favorite shapes, like Santa, crosses, and guns. Fold the liner cloth over, and put the top of the mold in place. Weigh down the tofu with an American can of chicken soup to remind the Japanese tofu of what can happen to them when they try to stick it to America. The just-pressed tofu will be very delicate (like some people we see on TV), so it will need time to firm up like a true American. Before removing the tofu from its mold, partially fill a bowl with cold water. Submerge tofu in the water for about five minutes to firm up. Store to keep it cool. You'll love how all your little shapes of tofu come out. The texture will be perfect and the consistency will be just right to enjoy with any of your Japanese dishes and delights.

Presentation

You can make all kinds of meals with tofu. Did you know soy beans are the number one genetically modified food in the world? For 20 years the big pharma folks have changed our bean. That's not good. They're poisoning our people slowly with their modified product just so they can make a buck. This process is called GMO. Genetically Modified Organism. These things are created in a frickin lab. They insert a gene from one organism and put it in a totally different organism. They're making plants and animals that never would be seen in God's nature. So, we'll probably all get allergies, kidney/liver disease, kids will continue to be diagnosed with attention deficit, cancer, our sperm and eggs won't work right anymore, immune disorders and I'm sure a lot more. I don't eat soy. Ever! If you do, there are meals called kimchi, atsuage, sushi, tempura, udon, and other interesting stuff. The Japanese make dishes that aren't just a bunch of crap thrown together. They're hard-working and creative people who constantly are looking at ways of improvement. They don't ask for handouts or reparations from the USA for acts that happened in the past. They came to the US, got their citizenships, worked their asses off, sent their kids to school, and helped improve the United States of America. No bullshit people who also know how to cook.

Japanese udon

Ingredients

1.2 L chicken broth
10 shiitake mushrooms, fresh
1 tablespoon canola oil
120 mL carrots, sliced
1 green onion, cut into 3-cm pieces
3 slices peeled fresh ginger, minced
3 cloves garlic, minced
1 tablespoon soy sauce
60 mL sake or rice wine
3 boneless chicken breasts
Black pepper, dash
Koshering salt, dash
425 grams udon noodles
8 slices hard-boiled egg
5 green onions, diagonally cut
284 grams baby bok choy, cut into 4 sections

Instructions

Cook the chicken in a saucepan till done. Shred the chicken with 2 forks. Remove stems from mushrooms and save them. Thinly slice the mushroom caps. Combine stems, ginger slices, crushed garlic, and green onions in a large saucepan with the chicken broth. Bring to a boil, cover, reduce heat and simmer for 20 minutes. Turn off heat and let stand for 10 minutes. Strain the broth through a sieve over a bowl.

This is basically just regular chicken soup with ginger and some strange fat noodle. Whatever. I would just make regular American chicken noodle soup, but if you want to be all international and cool, go ahead. Heat a large saucepan over medium-high heat. Add the canola oil, sliced mushroom caps, and carrots to the pan, and cook for 2 minutes. Add minced ginger and garlic and cook for 1 minute. Then put in sake, and cook for an additional 4 minutes. Apply the chicken broth, bring to a boil, and reduce heat to medium-low. Put in some soy sauce and pepper. Add shredded chicken and bok choy, simmer for 2 minutes. On the side, boil some water and cook the udon noodles for 10-12 minutes, then drain.

Presentation

Put the noodles in a bowl for each guest, then pour the broth mixture over the top. Throw in some green onion slices and serve with the sliced egg. Udon noodles are chunky wheat noodles that you typically find in Japanese cuisine. One time, this Japanese dude was eating across from me. He just slurped up the soup holding the bowl to his mouth and using the wood chop sticks to shove the solid contents down his throat. Interesting. Wow, udon. So cool. Big deal. Let's move on.

Chapter 6

Foods From Our Cold War Enemies

USSR beef stroganoff

Ingredients

2 kg beef tenderloin tips, cut in 1 cm cubes
2 tablespoons salted butter,
1 kg button mushrooms, sliced
1 onion, medium diced
2 tablespoons unbleached all-purpose flour
240 mL beef broth
1/2 tablespoon ground mustard seed
89 mL heavy cream
120 mL sour cream
1/2 teaspoon salt
1/4 teaspoon ground black pepper
1 kg egg noodles

Instructions

Boil a pot of water with some salt in it and cook the egg noodles till done, about 7 minutes. Drain. Toss the beef tips in flour and then cook the tenderloin tips in butter in a skillet, searing on all sides. Remove and set aside. Add diced onions to the pan and cook slightly. After a few minutes, add the mushrooms and cook till the mushrooms are dry. I forgot, while you're doing all of this, send your family down to the local bread line and have them wait with all the other poor, 15-hour a day working, starving socialist assholes who thought it'd be a good idea to get rid of capitalism and instill communism in the blessed and prosperous US of A. Add the beef broth, bring to a boil, reduce heat and simmer for 5 minutes. Put the sour cream and heavy cream into a small bowl and mix a bit of the broth from the skillet to warm it. Add the warmed sour cream mixture into the saucepan. Add the mustard and parsley. Return the beef to the pan and cook for a few minutes.

Presentation

How did this get so popular in our country anyway? I'll tell you how. After World War II, the left peace fuckheads in our United States were fooled by the ally deception of the USSR. Our greatest general, George S Patton, wasn't. He wanted to keep going through that snow-ridden land and wipe out those commie bastards. Too bad no one listened to him. Russia was seen as our friend. What a con job! We brought their easy-to-make stroganoff comfort food right to our doorsteps. It even infiltrated our school cafeterias. So, we might as well continue to play the role of the fool once again. Hello, the Cold War is still going on. Communism is creeping its way back into the United States. Are you going to be aware of this? Are you going to do something about it? Well, if you're not, invite over your closest Russian and

Chinese friends and enjoy this Eastern-bloc comfort dish and talk about the failures of capitalism and the American way. Oh, in Russia, you will most often find traditional beef stroganoff served over shoestring fries or mashed potatoes or rice.

Chinese stir fry

Ingredients

The main part
2 kg of good sirloin beef
1 tablespoon light soy sauce
2 teaspoons vegetable oil
50 g young ginger
4 stalks scallion
1 teaspoon sesame oil

Beef marinade:
1 and ½ tablespoons oyster sauce
1 teaspoon light soy sauce
1 teaspoon of salt
1 teaspoon sugar
1/4 teaspoon ground white pepper
1/2 teaspoon corn starch
4 tablespoons water

Instructions

Sirloin is best for stir frying. The meat should be cut into small pieces for beef stir-fry and marinated in the marinade for at least 15 minutes.

How to peel and cut ginger: get some kids about 7-9 years old and have them show up at 7 in the morning and work all day and night for a whopping 2 bucks a day. Ya. This is some really screwed-up child abuse that's happening in communist countries. Look at China. Their symbol is a hammer and sickle. Sound familiar? Yep, it's a far-left symbolism from the far east. Drives me nuts! Do the slicing yourself. Use a peeler to scrape away the skin, then use the edge of a metal spoon to scrape away any other part of the skin between the nubs. A sharp paring knife is best to slice the ginger thinly. Cut the scallion into pieces about 4 cm in length then slice the scallion lengthwise into fine strands.

This will be great. We're going to reproduce the powerful inferno of restaurant burners at home. Here's what you need: get 8 blow torches and tape together with duct tape. Make sure the bottoms are flat so they can rest on your stove top. Place a sheet of plywood over the stove. Get out your biggest wok, some pot holders, and maybe a stepstool to make sure your wok can get on top of the hottest part of the flame. Open up the blowtorches and light 'em up. Boom! (no pun intended) We've got some serious firestorm cooking happening. You're gonna need to hold the wok over the flame for a bit, so I hope you're strong enough. Heat up the wok with a little oil. Now cook the ginger and scallion for a couple of minutes. Push the ginger and scallion to the edge of the wok, add the meat in a single layer and let it sear for a while, then start tossing like crazy. Add the sesame oil, mix all together, and serve.

Presentation

Stir frying originated in China, and in recent centuries, has spread into other parts of Asia and made its migration all the way to the West. Yes, the cold war is on. What, do you think just because the Berlin wall came down that Russia and China haven't been plotting their takeover. See, they want us to fall from within. They've even gotten to our politicians. I wonder what those commies offered our American representatives in return. These people influenced by the ways of China are not smart people. Well, I guess we were fooled, because we put them as leads of our country. Places like China and other ant-American habitations around the world don't like us. They're jealous of our way of life. Well, when you give up your American way of life, you'll be eating stir fry with those silly wooden chop stick things the rest of your life. Let's set an example for our children by working hard, going to church, respecting one another, and knowing and appreciating that we live in the best fucking country on God's great planet. We'll show them the blueprint for long periods of prosperity You can use other types of meat with stir fry, like chicken, fish, and shrimp. They're all very tasty.

North Vietnamese bun cha

Ingredients

Main part of this
450 grams pork shoulder or pork belly
450 grams ground pork
50 grams shallots (about 6)
15 grams garlic (3 to 5 cloves)
Fish sauce and oyster sauce
Tiny pickles
400 grams green papaya, sliced carrots, kohlrabi
25 grams sugar
15 ml rice vinegar
Fresh coriander, perilla, lettuce, Vietnamese balm
0.5 kg dried rice noodles

Caramel sauce
70 grams sugar and 150 ml hot water

Dipping sauce
25 grams sugar
15 – 18 ml lemon juice
15 mL rice vinegar
175 ml water
15 – 20 ml fish sauce
Garlic, chili
Sliced papaya

Instructions

Holy shit, is that enough stuff? For the pork marinade, mix the water, sugar, fish sauce, garlic, and shallot together. Mix in both kinds of pork. After marinating separate the meats. Put the rice powder in the ground pork and make little nuclear missile patties. Grill the pork shoulder. I really don't care how. Fry up the pork missiles in a frying pan. Cook the noodles for 5 minutes in boiling water.

Now, make the dipping sauce. Add salt to the sliced papaya. Let it sit. Combine the hot water and sugar. Mix till dissolved. Add the rest of the crap and the papaya. Simply heat the sugar in the water to make the caramel sauce.

Presentation

Yes. These are famously called 'Obama noodles', since a certain someone visited Vietnam and ate the dish in 2016. It was a huge turning point for our initiative to victory in the Cold War. Not. Arrange the meats, rice noodles, aromatic herbs and romaine salad in a large dish. Place a series of small bowls with sauce, one with a few slices of carrots, another with turnips, and the last with green papaya. Bun cha. Ya. A buncha bullshit. Make sure you arrange the missile patties to target any free countries within range. Poor over the caramelized sauce to make it sweet. That's right, sweeten the true threat we face right now. Actually, no self-respecting American citizen would ever make this dish. Sure, we should treat everyone equally. In the USA we do. Take a trip to North Vietnam and you'll see just how the communist people live.

North Korean bosintang

Ingredients

3 kg dog meat
Vinegar
Peppercorns, crushed
6 tablespoons salt
12 cloves garlic, crushed
Cooking oil
2 onions, sliced
750 mL tomato sauce
2.4 L boiling water
5 red peppers, cut into strips
6 pieces of bay leaf
1 teaspoon tabasco sauce
Liver spread. Fuck it. Just make this from the dog
1 whole fresh pineapple, cut 1 cm thick

Instructions

That's right. These communist socialist jerks eat dog. Yep, dog. What the hell?! How could anyone ever go out, capture a dog, look it in its beautiful innocent eyes, and slaughter the little thing just to make some damn soup. OK. Cook the dog, however you do that, and add all the other shit in. We're friends with these people? Absolutely unacceptable! This is disgusting.

Presentation

Fuck all this shit! Now, I'm pissed off. We have the greatest country in the world. We also have the greatest pets! Yes, dogs and cats! We don't eat them. We love them. How can we let these cold-hearted bastards build their military and weapons of mass destruction right under our noses? Our government needs to get a spine and do something about this! This is what happens when left-minded value-lacking people start pushing down the core values of our country. While we're putting up with the gobbledygook of the outspoken and wrongly accusing left, the evil of the east is building a war powerhouse. Oh, the politicians will lie to you. The lefty followers will wrongly accuse you of something that doesn't make sense. Do not bear false witness is one of God's top ten rules that Moses brought down for us. This includes falsely speaking on any subject, lying, deceiving or devising and designing to deceive our good Americans, speaking unjustly, damaging reputations, and not being honest. Shame on those who break this commandment. These are the Ten Commandments that are not even spoken of anymore. The left media won't mention it. They even try to suppress it. Kind of like our Constitution! Shit, I hear more about sharvia law (or however the fuck you spell it) on the news and media than about our own commandments. So, leave man's best friend alone and make a regular American dish that all your fellow commandment followers will enjoy and love.

Chapter 7

Foods From Our
Desert Enemies

Arabian Sea naan

Ingredients

1 tablespoon sugar
2 teaspoons active dry yeast
1 egg
1/4 cup warm water
1/2 cup warm milk
1/2 cup plain yogurt
4 cups all-purpose flour
1 teaspoon salt
1/4 cup melted butter, for brushing
4 cloves minced garlic

Instructions

In a large glass bowl, dissolve yeast in warm water. Let it stand for about 10 minutes. Whisk in yogurt, sugar, milk, egg, salt, and flour. Knead for 7 minutes on a lightly floured surface. Tell the kids to come in after they've finished with their machete instructions from the neighborhood communist liaison. Remember, communists are the best terrorist teachers the world has ever seen. Place dough in an oiled bowl, cover with a damp cloth, and set aside to rise. While you're at it, cover all the women with a damp cloth, too. Let it rise 1 hour, till the dough has doubled in volume. I know these people are big fans of unleavened bread, but who the hell wants that. At least this has yeast! Ah, give me a piece of regular sliced white bread any day.

Punch down the dough and knead in the garlic. Pinch off small handfuls of dough about the size of a camel turd. Roll into balls, and place on a tray. Cover this with a towel. Let it rise till doubled in size, probably about 30 minutes. During the second rising, preheat grill to high heat. I wish there was a second rising of the alt-left that brought about the elevation of intelligence and due diligence. Put each ball on a floured surface. Knead into a disc. Repeat.

Heat a large skillet over medium heat. Brush the dough lightly with butter and place one at a time onto the hot skillet. Cook till large bubbles form on the surface. Flip the dough and cook the other side till golden, about 1-2 more minutes. Stack the cooked flat bread on a plate and again (bajesus) cover with a towel to keep warm as you cook the remaining pieces.

Presentation

This naan thing is good with smushed chick peas crap called hummus. Something called tahini sauce is in it, too. Do you know the difference between a chick pea and a garbanzo bean? It's a funny joke. Look it up. Anyway, put some kind of spread you like on your naan and have a delicious afternoon. Go America!

Afghan kabuli palaw

Ingredients

2 handfuls of camel meat
2 handfuls of basmati rice
Handful of golden raisins and carrots
2 medium onions, chopped
A cup of vegetable oil
3 cups of mutton broth
2 spoonfuls of cumin and cardamom
1/4 spoonful of black pepper and salt
1 spoonful of butter

Instructions

Slice carrots. Cook the carrots and raisins in butter and set aside. Now, heat the oil and cook onions for roughly 6 minutes. Boil mutton broth, add rice and cook on low for 12 minutes. Go out to your neighborhood trading post and barter your ammunition and terrorist weapons for a nice camel. Cut the camel in 1-inch cubes. I like to use meat from a 2-hump camel. The meat from these fluffy mammals seem to better than the one-hump variety. In another pan, heat some oil and fry all the spices with the camel. Add some salt and cook for 5 to 6 minutes. In a greased baking dish, put the camel pieces in the center and cover with half-done rice. I wonder if the sand people grease their leaders over there like some assholes do here? Spread the carrots and raisins on top. Preheat the oven on 250 degrees F and bake for about 20 minutes. Yummy.

Presentation

Who really cares? But let's get something straight. The people of Afghanistan get a lot of blame for terrorist acts around the world. I got news for you, it ain't the regular people. It's the psycho nut jobs running around with their faces covered. These are criminals. If Afghanistan let a big ole group of people from New York into their country, would they let 'em in if they were a group of weapons using, bomb building, ant-Afghanistan criminals? Hell no. The regular people there try to get out of Afghanistan as fast as they can. It's dangerous there. A bunch of vicious offenders run the place and make everyone's life miserable. This was especially true after the Russians took them over. See a pattern again? The communists have a solid habit of turning a place into a center of violent acts and hatred. What do they give back in return? Poverty and sadness. Then they move on to other countries and create more criminal waves of savages. Now, there are bad groups of attackers all over the world. They only seek to destroy righteous and hard-working people. It's bad. So, give thanks to our men and women in uniform who help preserve our beautiful American way of life, liberty, and the pursuit of happiness.

Somali suqaar

Ingredients

1 pound of stray or non-working mammal
1 tablespoon oil
1 onion, diced
2 tablespoons tomato puree
1/2 red capsicum, chopped into small pieces

Instructions

Heat the olive oil over medium heat in a pan. Dice the mammal meat into small cubes. Add the meat and a pinch of salt to the pan. Put in the onion, tomato puree, and capsicum. Cook the meat for a few minutes. Remove from heat.

Presentation

I usually go to the beach for fun. Maybe too much sun makes some of these people go crazy. I'm sure there are a lot of great people there. Too bad they're subdued by the asshole extremists! I have an idea, give all the fucking crazy people power and weapons. Have all the normal people barely get by. Have all the honest people locked into silence. Hide the truth. Exploit the lies. The hell with that. This is a simple meal you can make when you're in a hurry. Capsicum, if you're wondering, is a pepper. Maybe bring the dish to the beach for an international picnic? Maybe not.

Chapter 8

Meals for Those Who are Incapable of Eating Meat

Boring broccoli with mushrooms

Ingredients

1 pound broccoli floret
6 ounces Shiitake mushrooms, fresh
1 tablespoon vegetable oil
1 tablespoon sesame oil
2 teaspoon garlic, chopped
~~1 ounce oyster sauce~~ (oysters are animals)
Crushed red chilis

Instructions

Wash the broccoli and the mushrooms. Cut the broccoli into 1 to 2-inch pieces. Slice off the stems and cut the mushrooms into 1/2-inch pieces. Put some oil in a skillet and heat on medium. Add the garlic and stir-fry for a few seconds. Put in the sesame oil. Add the mushrooms and broccoli and cook for 1 minute. Pour in ~~the oyster sauce and add~~ the red chilis. Cook for about 4 minutes. The broccoli should be firm but not raw. The mushrooms will be dried a bit but not too dry. This is a very tasty combination that you and your foo foo friends will really like to eat.

Presentation

Ah, the vegan. Very impressive. I have an idea. If you want a disciplined cooking and diet regimen, try Kosher. These people know how to follow rules. Plus, you don't hear about their diet all the time. Ever meat (I did that on purpose) a vegan? You'll know in the first 3 sentences. Trust me. No hard-working American really gives a shit about how you eat. Or, especially, about how you're saving animals. Give me a frickin break.

I got news for you… animal fats and oils are separated from that animal that's gonna get slaughtered for your leather couch and shoes anyway. Vegetable oils are chemically extracted from plants. So, you're putting more chemicals in your body if you eat vegetable oils.

Plus, you're probably eating tons of soy. This shit is genetically altered. You also take vitamins and supplements for protein, I would suppose. You're not helping yourself. You're not helping any animals. You're not helping anything. More bullshit. Why don't you do some work for once and help out your community? We see right through you. So, eat your mushrooms and broccoli and post pictures of your dinner at that fancy restaurant with leather seats, more meat dishes than a local butcher, plates made in China, credit cards made in China, napkins and tablecloths that take millions of gallons of water and detergents to clean each week, and on and on. This stir fry is very tasty and also can be substituted or complemented with a number of fresh vegetables. Oh, and compliment the vegan, too. They need it.

Safe space butternut squash

Ingredients

1/2 pound butternut squash
1/8 teaspoon cinnamon
1/16 teaspoon cardamon
1 tablespoon brown sugar
1 tablespoon lemon juice
1 ounce whole butter
Salt
Pepper

Instructions

Heat oven to 350 degrees F. Scoop out the meat part of the squash. Notice how I used meat there? I'll probably get a bad review, because some veg-head reads meat in the meatless section. Dice the squash in 1/2-inch cubes. Put in a casserole dish. Season with salt and pepper, cinnamon, cardamom, and brown sugar. Drizzle a little lemon juice over the squash. Cook it uncovered for about 50 minutes. Oh, make sure you take the seeds and plant them in the forest so you can tell your grandkids you grew a squash tree. They'll be so proud of you. Most importantly, you'll be so proud of yourself and the great contribution you have made to the world. See a lot of people like to publicize any good deed they think they've done. There's something called being humble that many have seem to have forgotten. It's stupid and annoying these animated people.

Presentation

Have some squash then go play some squash. You won't be full, at all, from this veggie dish so at least you can get some friends and go do an activity. Squash is played like racquetball in a court surrounded by walls. Not the kind of court that's gonna sentence you to jail for having a legal gun. A court of play. They call it squash because when you hit the ball, it gets squashed. Just like all your rights are gonna get squashed as all your fellow do-gooders go out and spend all their time protesting amendments that were established to protect the American people from a big and tyrannical government. Some people just don't get it, do they? Who has all this time to protest anyway? Don't these people have jobs and families to care for? Where's the responsibility? I call boloney, again! You can just cut the squash in half, put in on a cooking sheet, scoop out all the seeds and stringy stuff, put all the goodies on top, and put the halves on a cooking sheet. Bake it at 350 F for about 37 minutes and it'll come out perfectly.

Communist red cabbage with red apples and red wine

Ingredients

12 ounces red cabbage
1 red apple
~~3 bacon strips~~ (Oops I did it again. Wouldn't want to offend anyone!)
1 red onion
1 ounce vegetable oil
2 ounces red wine
~~2 ounces chicken stock~~ (Damnit)
1/4 of a cinnamon stick
1 teaspoon brown sugar
1 tablespoon cider vinegar
Salt
Pepper

Instructions

Shred the cabbage and dice the apple and onion. ~~Cook the bacon in the oven at 350 degrees F for about 15 minutes, chop up, and add to the cabbage if you want this dish to taste any good.~~ Heat oil in a skillet. Cook onions for a few minutes. Add the cabbage and cook for

5 minutes. Season with salt and pepper. Add the wine, ~~chicken stock~~, brown sugar, vinegar and cinnamon stick. Mix it up. Cover and braise for about 40 minutes. After that, add the apples, cover and continue to braise for 5 minutes.

Presentation

What can I say? It's cabbage and apples. Whipty doo!

Talking in circles fried onions

Ingredients

7 onions
1/2 an egg (what is a half an egg you say?)
2 ounces flour
1/2 teaspoon baking powder
Salt
White pepper
3 ounces American beer

Instructions

Beat the egg in a bowl and pour out half of it. See? Half an egg. Oh shit. An egg isn't vegan, is it? Well if you can't eat an unfertilized thing in a shell then just skip this step. The breading may not stick to the onions, but you're probably not used to eating anything of substance anyway. Add in the 3 ounces of beer. Drink the rest. Mix in the flour, baking powder, salt, and white pepper. You should probably mix and sift the dry ingredients first. Peel the onions and cut into cool sickle-like slices for that communist touch. Now heat up the oil to 375 F. Drop the sickles in. They'll float on the oil. You're gonna have to flip them at some point. When they're done, drain on some absorbent paper. Add a dash of salt and pepper and that'll give it just enough seasoning. The onions and breading create all the taste in these little flavorful snacks. Plus, you can always dunk these in ketchup or something like that.

Presenation

Place the onion slices on a flat plate in your favorite religious symbol. There are plenty of them... triangles, circles, squares, stars, etc. I prefer the cross, but use whatever you think is right. Or if you're really on the communist bend, pour some ketchup on the plate in a rectangle, put the onion slices in the upper left-hand corner. Make one big 5-point star and 4 smaller stars. You did it. China flag. Here's what your communist flag means: the larger star is the communist party. The itty-bitty stars are the people. Yep. The new democracy of the left. Embrace it, jerks. For the rest of us Americans, place those onion rings on the steaks you cooked for your family, or they also go great with hamburgers on the grill. I love onion rings. I love my family and friends. They're great people who work hard. They support the USA. They support police. They support the brave soldiers of our military, they support freedom, they support life. I've had enough of these vegetarian fake freedom fighters trying to push their agenda on us good people. Stand strong Americans. If you want to eat meat, eat it. Vegetables are sides. They support meat. They don't run off on their own and oppose the meats. See vegetables from the ground are smarter and more dedicated than the vegetables who are so dumb that they aimlessly follow the leadership that will eventually lead them to their doom. Remember the phrase, "If they told you to jump off a bridge, would you?" Hell, most of these mindless bastards would say yes! Or would change the subject and talk about the importance of a vegetarian diet. My goodness. Is there hope for these people? Hope you like the onion rings.

Chapter 9

Desserts

American-made turtles

Ingredients

8 ounces pecan halves, roasted
25 caramel squares
1/4 cup cream
16 ounces roughly chopped chocolate, melted
Sea salt, optional for sprinkling

Instructions

Line parchment paper on your counter. Set 5 pieces of pecans together in the shape of a turtle. See, turtles create their own safe space. They don't need someone to frickin' do it for them. Self-made. Strong. In a medium pot, add the caramels, half of the cream, and heat on low to melt. Stir the mixture every 30 seconds so you don't burn it. Add about 1 tablespoon caramel to the top of each pecan turtle. In another pot, add 8 ounces chocolate and the rest of the cream. Heat to melt. Stir constantly. Add about 2 tablespoons chocolate to the top of each pecan turtle. You can also add a pinch of sea salt. Allow turtles to firm up at room temp or in the fridge. At room temperature it might take a few hours. I always put them in the fridge. I don't have time to wait for little treats. They're delicious.

Presentation

Aren't they cute? They look like those little antifa protestors with their comical riot suits on. Ha! So, line them up on the counter in the militant group formation and have your family and friends eat them down one bite at a time. How fun will that be?

Factual fruit smoothie

Ingredients

2 cups of your favorite fruit
2 cups ice

Instructions

Put it all in a blender and grind away. You can add some milk or ice cream, too. It'll make a creamy, blessed treat for those hot days. The Fourth of July is a hot day. What a wonderful day that is. I just love it. Everyone's so happy and full of life. I wonder what anti-Americans do on the Fourth of July. Oooo… we should make flag tissues for them. We can make the box look like the flag, too. They'll probably cry the entire day. Or maybe they go to the movies and watch their favorite leftist highly political talking beyond their knowledge actress or actor. Who would listen to a person who has the profession of performing? Essentially, they lie for a living by representing someone or something that is not them. Silly stuff here. I like to make my smoothies super thick so you almost have to eat it with a spoon. Or you can suck it up. Through a straw. You don't actually suck, you create a vacuum, but that's for another time and place and subject to discuss with you.

Presentation

Put in a glass. Drink. There's no need add chia seeds, whey protein, vitamins, or some other crazy supplemental concoction that they process and sell to the public claiming all these wonderful health benefits. It's fruit and ice for goodness sakes. You're gonna get your nutrients. Americans spend billions of dollars on supplements every year. How stupid is that. They don't do anything regular foods don't do. Where the hell do you think they get the supplemental nutritional entities anyway? From plants and animals. This facade of regular Americans needing to take all of these chemical powders, pills, and drinks is getting out of hand. Don't be a dummy. Eat like our predecessors ate. Cook your own food, grow your own food, and get the most natural meats and vegetables you can. It's easy. Take it from our ancestors who worked physical labor for hours and hours throughout their lifetimes. They were healthy and confident. Good basic American standards to live by.

Our homemade ice cream

Ingredients

3 cups heavy cream
1 cup whole milk
1 cup sugar
1 tablespoon pure vanilla extract
1/2 teaspoon koshering salt
5 egg yolks

Instructions

Whisk the cream, milk, sugar, vanilla and 1/2 teaspoon salt in a medium saucepan and bring to a simmer over medium heat. On the side, beat the egg yolks in a medium bowl. Slowly pour 1 cup of the hot cream mixture into the yolks. Now pour that back into the saucepan. Cook, stirring constantly with a wooden spoon, till the mixture thickens. It'll be 180 degrees F. Remove from the heat and strain the custard through a sieve into a bowl. Keep stirring till the mixture cools to room temperature. If you want it fruity, puree berries in a blender or food processor and stir into the other ingredients before freezing. If you want to make rainbow ice cream, try putting your colors in. Guess what? It'll come out brown. Not the delicious brown color of chocolate ice cream. Brown like dirt. Rainbow ice cream is made by doing all the flavors separately, then at the end, placing each flavor next to each other. Jeez. Put a 13x9-inch glass dish in the freezer till cold. Put the custard in the dish and press some plastic wrap on the surface of the custard to prevent skin from forming. Freeze till the edges begin to set, probably 20-30 minutes. Freeze, covered, till firm, about 3 hours longer. Make sure you whisk it every 30 minutes.

Presentation

Yes! Ice cream time. Let's have an ice cream social. No not a socialist kind of social. American has been having these fun events for last 2 centuries. They're great times. Get some sprinkles or chopped up candy bars, cover that delicious bowl or cone of ice cream, and have a blast! Hell, if you're a real douche bag, have a fundraiser with it. Left heads love fundraisers, so they can just throw their money away to some unknown money holder who will just use the cash for their own climb up the ladder. You know what? Fuck that. Just have a good ole American fun time with family and friends. God bless America!

God bless all of you, my loving and dedicated Americans!